TEMPT

(a *Take It Off* novel)

Stranded and alone with not one, but two wickedly enticing men.

Ava arrives at the airport, expecting to board a commercial flight to Puerto Rico. But a plane ticket isn't waiting for her. Instead, she finds a guy with dark curly hair wearing seriously ratty jeans and holding a sign with her name on it.

He may not look like a pilot, but he is. And he's her ride.

So now it's just Nash and her on a tiny tin can of a plane flying over the Atlantic. When a thunderstorm comes out of nowhere, it proves to be too much for the little aircraft.

Ava and Nash plunge from the sky and end up on an uncharted deserted island.

Stranded.

As if that isn't bad enough, Ava starts to desire more than just rescue—hunger for more than food. Nash is only too happy to oblige… but it seems they might not be as alone as they thought.

And Nash might have some competition in claiming Ava's body… and her heart.

TEMPT

Take It Off Series

CAMBRIA HEBERT

Published by: Cambria Hebert

http://www.cambriahebert.com

Interior design and typesetting by Sharon Kay
Cover design by MAE I DESIGN
Edited by Cassie McCown
Copyright 2013 by Cambria Hebert

Paperback ISBN: 978-1-938857-30-0
eBook ISBN: 978-1-938857-31-7

DEDICATION

To Regina Wamba. We started out as designer/client and we grew to be colleagues and friends. Your designs inspire and awe me. One of the best decisions I ever made when I started writing was hiring you to give my books beautiful faces.

Beyond that, this book is for you because you're the one who titled it.

TEMPT

PROLOGUE

I felt my heartbeat against my chest—a slow, steady rhythm, kind of lethargic and lazy. But that was because I was barely breathing. Actually, I was holding my breath.

He touched me.

His fingers drifted over my skin like a breeze on a summer day. It was a feather-light caress that never ended because he didn't lift his hands.

It started at my collarbone, drifted out across my shoulders, and then descended downward until he hooked his fingers around my elbow, brushing against the sensitive spot on the inside of my arm. Downward he traveled until his fingers pulled away from mine to hover just barely over the tops of my thighs.

Then his direction reversed, climbing upward so the slightly rough pads of his fingers traced the outline of my belly button and then dragged over my ribcage.

Tiny shivers raced up and down my spine, creating goose bumps that scattered over my scalp and caused my eyes to flutter closed.

His hands splayed around my waist, gripping my flesh and pulling me closer, but he didn't kiss me. He buried his face against my neck and used his tongue to wet a circle of tender skin, then pulled back slightly to blow across the area.

I shuddered.

My body started to arch into him, but something caught my arm, something large and warm. It wrapped around my bicep in a possessive manner, causing my head to turn, and I cast a glance in the direction I was being pulled.

My heartbeat accelerated instantly. The lethargic rhythm was chased away by a shot of adrenaline so pure that I could taste it on my tongue.

He yanked me away from the teasing, gentle caresses and cupped my face in his palm, lowering his lips toward mine. Excitement crackled along my nerve endings, and my tongue jutted out to moisten my lips.

Just as he was about to claim my kiss, I was yanked away again, this time by the one who had me first.

I cast a look to my left at green irises flashing with possession and then once again to my right where chocolate eyes gleamed with jealousy.

I was caught in the middle of two very enticing choices.

A choice I didn't want to make.

Brown-eyes stepped closer, his body brushing against the entire length of my arm. He reached out and pushed the hair back over my shoulder, exposing the side of my face. He leaned down and captured my earlobe between his teeth and sucked it into his mouth. The gentle suckling sounds that whispered through my ear loosened something deep inside me.

I turned my head toward him, not wanting him to stop.

But green-eyes was not to be cast aside.

His palm covered my breast, gently kneading the area and causing my hardening nipple to brush against the smooth fabric of my bikini top. And then his mouth was on my neck, pulling the skin into its moist warmth and massaging it with his tongue.

Two mouths...

Two sets of hands...

And my single body.

I wasn't sure who to touch, who to grab, but I didn't want either of them to stop. The sensation of being kissed in more than one place in a single moment made a moan escape from my lips.

My fingers began to twitch, wanting to elicit a shiver of their own.

As my hands lifted away from my sides, I vaguely wondered whom they would reach for first...

1

Scientists, philosophers, or whoever the group of people who sat around a desk and made up the list of the Seven Wonders of the World were wrong. There aren't seven. There are eight.

Number eight being men.

The reason men weren't added as a wonder of the world? Because men probably made up the list to begin with.

I knew trying to figure out men, trying to have one in my life was a fruitless effort, but it didn't stop me from having a relationship. It also didn't stop me from getting hurt.

Just when I was getting over the epic failure that was my ex, my grandmother died.

So basically, I felt like I'd boxed about ten rounds, the entire time holding my own, and then I was knocked out. Cold.

And now here I was, wandering through the insanely large, insanely busy Miami International Airport so I could get on some plane and fly off to

Puerto Rico because my grandmother's dying wish was for her ashes to be scattered over the ocean there—the place where she met my grandfather over fifty years ago.

How did I get elected for the job?

I was Grandmother's favorite. I was between jobs. I was down on my luck. I needed a free vacation to a beautiful place.

Right. Because flying to some foreign country (though, I guess technically, it's not a foreign country since it's considered a US territory) with a special suitcase just for the remains of my beloved grandmother and then parting with them to an ocean is considered some nice vacation.

Clearly, my family is a bunch of whackos.

Even still, I love my family and my heart still ached over my grandmother's passing, so here I was. The suitcase rolling along behind me tipped, and my bags toppled to the floor. With a great sigh, I stopped and turned, righting the one on wheels and then bending over to pick up the one I had balanced on top.

I slid it over and unzipped it, peering inside at the bubble-wrapped urn. Nothing appeared to be broken. "Sorry, Kiki," I murmured, using the name I called her since I could speak, and then zipped it closed. Deciding not to take any more chances with the smaller bag, I carried on, rolling the bigger one behind and carrying the other in my free hand. I also had a messenger-style purse strapped across my shoulder and it banged against my thigh with every step.

I made my way through the rapidly moving crowds, toward the gate I was told would have my ticket. Why I couldn't get an electronic one like everyone else in the modern age I would never understand.

As I approached the gate, I couldn't help but be distracted by a man leaning against one of the nearby walls. He was reading a newspaper, holding it up in front of his face so all I could see were the two long-fingered hands holding the paper and his body from the waist down.

He wore a pair of beat-up jeans, really beat up. Like, with holes and hanging strings. The denim was faded in some spots and the fabric seemed thin and likely soft to the touch. His T-shirt looked as well worn as his jeans, except it didn't have any holes in it. All I could see of it was gray and just the front hem was tucked into his waistband, exposing a tan leather belt.

The way he leaned against the wall, kind of slouching with one foot out farther than the other, drew attention to his shoes. The boots were the same color as his belt and they appeared sturdy and not nearly as used as his clothes.

I couldn't tell you why I was so drawn to him. That was all I could see. He just looked like some regular (albeit lazy) guy waiting around for his plane to arrive. Although, he was reading the *New York Times,* which made me snort. He didn't really look like the kind of guy that would stand around reading that paper.

I snorted to myself again. He probably had a *Penthouse* just inside the paper and was really reading that.

My gate was off to my right and I turned, eyeing the counter and noting that there weren't as many people in this section of the airport as the other parts I'd just walked through. The woman behind the counter had perfectly combed hair slicked up into a bun on the back of her head. She was dressed in a navy blazer with the airline's name on the breast, and she sported a polite look on her face. When I stopped at the counter, I parked my bags next to me and flipped the top of my messenger bag open to reach inside for my wallet and ID.

"My name is Ava Malone. I was told my ticket to Puerto Rico would be here waiting for me."

The woman took my ID and looked at it and then handed it back to me. Her manicured fingers flew over the keyboard behind the counter and then she paused and looked up. "You're plane is already here."

Alarm spiked through me. "Am I late? I thought I was an hour early. As soon as I get my ticket, I'll go board. Will they hold the plane for me?"

She gave me an odd sort of look. "I'm sure it will wait, seeing as how you are the only passenger."

Confusion made me speechless. I felt my face scrunch up in an odd sort of way as her words replayed through my head. "I don't understand," I said slowly. "I can't be the only person flying to Puerto Rico today."

She shook her head. "Definitely not. But you are the only one who had a private plane come and fetch her."

A private plane? To fetch me?

"You must have the wrong person," I said, holding up my ID again. "You should check again. I should just have a ticket here. For one of the commercial flights."

"You're Ava Malone, correct?"

I glanced at my ID just to be sure. That's what it said, right there beside my horribly embarrassing photo. "Appears that's me," I muttered.

She smiled. "Your pilot is around here somewhere," she said, craning her neck to look around. Her eyes settled on someone across the room and she smiled. "He's right over there."

I turned, following her gaze. There next to the guy with ratty jeans was an older gentleman in a suit, holding a briefcase. I lifted my hand to wave at him. He got this puzzled look on his face and then waved uncertainly.

"Are you sure?" I said, feeling my cheeks heat with embarrassment as I glanced back at the woman.

I turned back around to glance again. The gentleman with the suit was gone. My eyes darted around, looking for him, but once again were drawn to the guy with the newspaper. He must have felt my stare because his head shot up and I saw his eyes peek over the top.

Slowly, the newspaper came down and something else was lifted. A giant white index card.

It had my name on it.

My stomach did a somersault and my heart started thumping erratically.

Why would that ratty jean wearing, *Penthouse* reading guy have a sign with my name on it?

"See," the woman said from behind. "That's him. He has a sign with your name on it."

"*That's* my pilot?"

The woman at the counter giggled. She actually giggled like a schoolgirl.

Shoot. Me. Now.

I gathered up my bags and took a few steps forward, intent on finding out just what the hell was going on, when he lowered the oversized card.

My steps faltered.

The suitcase trailing along behind me kept going and rammed into my calves, making me stumble, and I pitched forward with a startled cry, knowing I was going to go down and praying to the heavens that I didn't crush Kiki when I fell.

The last thing I saw was the stupid *New York Times* paper fluttering to the floor as Kiki and I plunged disastrously toward the floor. But then he was there, grabbing up the suitcase, saving it from my clumsiness.

I, however, was not so lucky.

I fell.

Hard. In fact, if my arms hadn't been free, I would have fallen directly on my face. Thankfully, my hands slapped against the hard floor, saving my nose from being rearranged. When I hit, I fell over, rolling onto my back, and lifted my hands, staring at them in front of my face. My palms stung from the fall and I cringed imaging how many germs were now crawling all over them from touching the nasty airport floor.

"Are you okay?" said a voice above me.

I jerked my arms down, propping myself up on my elbows, and lifted my eyes.

I remembered why I fell all over again.

Light-green eyes speared me from within a face that, even if he left right now and I never ever saw him again, I would not forget. His face was so striking that it would be etched into my mind forever.

His eyes were the color of green sea glass. A bright green but light because it had spent time tumbling around the ocean floor. They were a striking contrast against the rest of him. He was all dark and bronze with a head full of thick dark hair that curled around on his head. It was messy like he never combed it—though I would think that combing curls would only give him an Afro.

His skin was olive toned, bronzed like he never left the sun, and he had sharp features—a straight nose, full lips, and cheekbones that sat high just beneath those eyes, which were lined in impossibly thick, impossibly dark lashes.

He was tall (or maybe he just looked that way because I was sprawled on the floor) and had a lean build, but he looked strong—the kind of strength that came naturally, not the kind of bulk that came from the gym.

As I stared at him like a complete idiot, he set down the suitcase carefully and squatted beside me. My breath caught (or maybe I just forgot I needed to breathe) when he got closer. He was freaking beautiful. Yeah, I know, guys aren't supposed to be beautiful, but he was. There was no other word that I could think of that would describe him better.

I was still staring as he reached out and grasped me by the shoulders. The heat of his hands radiated through my T-shirt and practically zapped me back to reality. "Did you hurt yourself?"

Oh my God, he had an accent. It was lyrical and caused my tongue to tie itself in knots.

As if perfection just upped its game and got even better.

It wasn't a full-on Spanish accent, but barely there—a slight roll of the tongue that caused chills to rise up across my scalp and race over my head and down my spine.

I nodded because speaking was still not an option.

"You're Ava Malone?"

Say it again. Something inside me begged. *Please just say my name one more time.*

The desperation going on inside my own head was what fully shocked me out of my trance. There was no way I was about to succumb to some beautiful disaster of a man. And yes, I did know that he was a complete disaster because there was no way on this planet that a man who looked like him could be anything but trouble.

"Yes, that's me. I'm fine," I said, shaking off his hands and standing up. "Nice catch by the way." I gestured to the suitcase that contained Kiki.

He grinned. His teeth were blindingly white against his tanned skin. "Sorry, it had to be one or the other."

He didn't look sorry, the snake. He probably enjoyed watching me bust my butt. "Uh-huh," I said, reaching for the suitcase with the urn.

He reached out and took it first.

My back teeth clenched together.

"I can get my bags."

"After what I just saw, I think your grandmother would be safer in my arms."

That should have insulted me. It should have alarmed me that he knew what was inside. Instead, all I got was a vision of being tucked against his chest, with bronzed, strong arms wrapped around me and the beating of his heart beneath my ear.

I needed a drink.

[11]

A stiff one.

I pushed my raging thirst and apparent horniness to the back of my mind to say, "How did you know what was in there?"

"Was it a secret?" he asked, a little smile playing on his lips.

"Are you a psychic?"

He laughed. It was a warm, rich sound that reminded me of brewing coffee on a cold, early morning. "No. I'm not psychic. I'm just your ride."

"My ride?" I won't even describe the vision that floated through my mind when he said *that*.

He nodded like I was two. "Yes. Me, pilot. You, passenger." He pointed between us while he spoke.

"You're a pilot?"

He fished a pilot's license out of the back of his pocket and held it up. "That's what it says."

I scoffed. "I'm surprised that didn't fall out of the pocket of those holey pants."

His smile spread across his face like a slow, contagious disease. A disease that people would actually line up to catch. "My jeans hold in everything that's important."

I blushed.

Like, seriously.

To cover up my juvenile behavior, I squinted at the name on the license he was still holding up. "Nash Prescott," I read.

"At your service."

"You don't look old enough to be a pilot."

"You don't look old enough to travel alone."

I rolled my eyes.

"I'm twenty-three. I've been flying since I was a teenager. I've got more flight hours than you have hair on your head."

"Doubtful." I had really thick, long blond hair.

He cocked his head to the side and studied me. "Anyone ever tell you that you look like Kate Hudson?"

The actress? Daughter of Goldie Hawn. Actually, yes, they had. "Nope."

He smiled like he knew I was lying.

There was no way I was getting on a plane with him. "I'm sorry you had to come here all the way from… well, from wherever you came."

"Puerto Rico," he said, and when he did, his accent came out full force. It made the place sound exotic and enticing. "I flew here from Puerto Rico."

"You flew here to pick me up?"

He nodded.

"But why?"

"Our abuelas were great friends." He explained. "When your family called to arrange for her ashes to be scattered, my abuela offered for me to come and pick you up."

"So they volunteered you to come here like my family volunteered me to go there."

He smiled. "I guess both our families are loco." He used his pointer finger to draw circles around the side of his head.

I giggled. Then I sighed. "Look, I'm sorry you had to come here. I'll just go to the ticket counter and get a commercial flight and let you get back to your… whatever it is that you do."

"Right now my job is to take you to Puerto Rico, where you will stay with my grandmother and then be escorted to the place where you are to spread these ashes." He gestured toward the case in his hand.

"I'm supposed to stay with you?" I asked, feeling my eyes bug out of my head.

"Not me. My abuela."

"Abuela? That's Spanish for grandmother, right?"

He nodded.

"You don't live with her?"

He chuckled softly. "I think that would cramp my style."

Exactly. And why was I still here talking to him? I started to walk away. He stopped me. His hand was like a rope wrapping around my wrist. It was like a handcuff trapping me to a jail cell, a vise around my heart.

"*Esperate*," he said softly. The word literally rolled right off his tongue.

I turned back. You would've too.

My eyes locked on his, searching their translucent depths. "I really hope you didn't just insult me." Even if he did, I really didn't care. It was the sexiest insult I'd ever heard.

His smile was lopsided. I thought I might faint. "I said wait a second."

I glanced at his hand wrapped around my wrist, then back up. He saw me looking. He didn't let go. "There's no need for another ticket when I can take you."

I hesitated. What excuse could I give? I couldn't exactly say, "I'm sorry, but you are way too sexy for me to have to sit alone with on a plane for any amount of time." It wasn't like he drove a couple hours to pick me up. He freaking flew a plane to get me. He was doing it as a favor for his grandmother.

"How do I know you aren't really a kidnapper?"

"Two reasons," he said, releasing my arm.

I lifted an eyebrow.

"One," he said, holding up a finger. "I don't have to kidnap women. If I want one, I get one."

I actually believed that. He probably had women lined up at home.

"And two," he said, flicking up a second finger. "My abuela is Marisol Castillo."

Again, his accent was more pronounced when he spoke her name. A name that I recognized. She was indeed my grandmother's very dear friend.

"Your abuela is Marisol?"

He produced a picture from the same pocket where he kept his ID and held it out. It was of my grandmother, Cora, and Marisol. I had seen this same image hanging on her refrigerator practically all my life.

I took the photo out of his hands, staring down at Kiki with tears blurring my vision. I missed her. I missed her so much. "Okay," I said softly. "I'll go with you."

He reached around me with his free hand and took my rolling suitcase. "Let's go."

I trailed along behind him like a puppy, mentally telling myself I was going to regret this.

2

"You can't be serious," I said the second we stepped outside.

He glanced over his shoulder. "Isn't she a beauty?"

A tin can with wings? Yes. A sardine can with the words "death trap" scrawled across the side? You bet. A beauty? Hell to the no.

"I'm not riding in that thing."

"Why not?" he called, not even bothering to look back this time. He just kept right on strolling, putting one impossibly long leg in front of the other. (Turns out even after I stood up, he was still very tall.)

"That thing isn't even fit to fly!" I exclaimed, rushing after him.

"It got me here, didn't it?"

Somehow that did not make me feel better.

He kept moving, walking up the tiny set of stairs and into the plane, taking my luggage with him. I wasn't going up there.

Instead, I stood at the bottom of the stairs and yelled up. "Hey! I want my stuff back."

His curly dark head appeared out the door. "Come get it."

"You little…" I growled and stomped up the stairs.

I walked into the plane, noted my bags sitting in the first seat on the right, and went toward them. He closed the hatch (or whatever the door on a plane is called) behind me. I stiffened and turned. "Oh no. I'm getting off this death trap."

"It's not a death trap. You can get off when we get to Puerto Rico."

"Now."

"There's soda in the back if you want some."

"Do you not hear the words coming out of my mouth?"

"As soon as I have clearance, we can take off."

Why did I bother talking? I grabbed up my bags and walked to the door.

Just as I was pulling open the door, the plane's engine rumbled to life. I shut the door and glanced into the open cockpit. Nash looked over his shoulder at me and grinned. "Better buckle up."

When the plane started moving, I found a seat and definitely buckled up. If I was going to die, it would be safely. The plane taxied toward the runway and then stopped. I thought briefly of trying to escape, but then I decided against it. I was already here. Might as well take the ride.

I settled into the seat, trying not to think about the fact that the plane was so small it only had one row of seats on each side. I tried not to think about the fact there was no flight attendant to give instructions preflight about how to use the dropdown air masks. *Oh crap.* Did this plane even have those?

I pulled some gum out of my bag and popped it into my mouth. The worst part about flying was the ear popping. Gum would hopefully help that.

Everything was fine until we got into the air. This little plane didn't seem as sturdy as the commercial flights I'd been on. It seemed to teeter through the sky, bumping along, with us inside. Nerves kicked up inside me and I began to dread the rest of my time on this plane.

"Hey!" called a voice from the front.

I unbuckled my seatbelt and moved forward, peeking into the cockpit, my heart racing and my mind spinning theories of him having some weird emergency and needing me to fly the plane.

But he didn't appear to be in need of help.

He actually looked really relaxed and confident sitting in the pilot's chair. He had headphones over his ears, but one side was pushed back so it wasn't covering that ear. My eyes were drawn immediately to the windshield, or rather what was beyond it.

It was sort of like seeing the ocean, except there was no water and we weren't on the ground. But there was an endless supply of blue. An endless supply of completely bare and undisturbed landscape dotted with white clouds that looked impossibly soft and much more 3D up here than from the ground. I wondered what it would be like to reach out and touch one, if my fingers would slip right through it like vapor... or if it would have some sort of feel against my skin. Would it be silky and soft? Would it be slightly moist and warm? I knew I would likely never know what it felt like, but being up here made it very easy to imagine.

"Want to help?" Nash called from his seat.

"I don't know how to fly."

He motioned for the empty seat beside him. I moved over cautiously, gingerly perching on the edge. He laughed. "Isn't the view awesome?"

"It really is!"

"Want to steer?"

I shook my head. I wasn't about to try and steer. I'd probably manage to hit a bird or something.

He lifted his hands off all the controls. "Look! No hands!"

"Stop that!" I yelled, unable to cover up my smile.

"Come here," he said, motioning with his chin.

I moved around so I was standing right beside him. He hooked me around the waist and pulled, causing me to tumble right into his lap. I gave a little shriek and he laughed. "Put your hands over mine," he instructed.

I hesitated and then I reached up. Flying a plane was something I never thought I would do. Flying a plane while sitting in the lap of some hot guy? That thought never even crossed my mind.

I liked it.

I wrapped my hands around his, both of us gripping the controls. "Nice and easy," he murmured right next to my ear. "She practically drives herself."

My eyes momentarily fluttered closed. His warm breath brushing across my ear made me feel like I just had a thirty-minute massage. My body felt heavy and languid and I actually had to make a conscious effort to support my own weight and not give it all to him.

After a few minutes of flying together, he slipped his hands out from beneath mine and I was left to fly alone. I gave a squeal of excitement. "I'm flying!"

His laugh vibrated my ear and his arms fell loosely around my waist. If I leaned back, I would be encircled in his body…

The plane jerked a little and his hands came back up over mine. "Whoa," he said. "Easy."

"I think I better leave the flying to you."

I moved off his lap, returning to the vacant seat beside him. We flew in silence for a while. The scenery mesmerized me.

But then the clouds started to turn a darker color. They were no longer fluffy and white. Instead, they glowed a sort of electric gray color, and I swore I saw some lightning flashing here and there.

"What's happening?" I asked him, unease filling my body.

He was looking out the window with a confused look on his face. "It wasn't supposed to rain today."

"Rain?" Were we flying into bad weather?

He nodded. "You should go back and buckle up."

"Is everything okay?" I needed to know.

"Everything's fine." He assured me, but not before I caught the hesitation in his tone.

I did as he asked, heading back toward my seat. Just as I got there, we seemed to hit a pocket of turbulence and I fell over in the aisle, bumping my shoulder on the seat. I scrambled back up, sitting down and fumbling to fasten the belt around my waist.

At the moment, it seemed silly. Like a strip of fabric around my waist was really going to help me if this plane decided to plunge out of the sky. But I left it there anyway, thinking it couldn't hurt. Plus, in some ways, it was a comfort. It made me feel safer, even if I wasn't.

After a few minutes, the plane evened out and the flight grew smooth again. I let out a shaky breath and relaxed my stiffened muscles. I rolled my head to the side and glanced out the tiny oval window and into the sky.

It was dark.

The once-fluffy clouds now looked angry and dirty.

The plane seemed to tilt then and then rapidly righted once more. My stomach rolled. Turbulence rocked us again, and it felt as if we dropped about ten feet in a span of one second. I swallowed back the panic clawing at my throat.

Everything's fine.

It's just a storm.

I repeated that mantra over and over again until I lost track of time. The plane still struggled through the air and Nash didn't say a word. I didn't dare ask him what was happening. I didn't want to take away any of his concentration.

And then it started to rain. Huge, fat drops of water plastered against the little window and soaked the plane.

Over the sound of the pounding rain, I heard a muffled curse.

That's when I knew we were in trouble.

I scrabbled with the seatbelt, finally getting it undone, and raced toward the front. I felt like I was in some sort of carnival funhouse—the kind with a tilting floor that made it impossible to walk straight.

"Nash!" I yelled, rushing forward.

"Go back to your seat, Ava," he yelled, not looking away from the windshield. "I've got this under control."

I admired his confidence. I admired how assured he was. It almost made me feel better. Almost. But then I looked at the sweeping view before us.

It looked like we were flying right into the mouth of some kind of swirling, angry beast. I knew the wind was fierce because of the speed the uber-dark clouds scattering across the sky. The rain still pelted the plane, falling in heavy sheets so fast the tiny windshield wipers could barely keep up.

Blinding white lightning shot through the sky, lighting up portions of the storm. I understood now why some people said a thunderstorm was really the gods fighting. This was intense and powerful.

"Go sit," Nash barked.

I did as he asked because I didn't know what else to do. I'd never in my life felt so helpless than I did right then. It was like seeing a clear future toward imminent death and not being able to do a thing to stop it.

I started to pray. I said every prayer I knew and then I closed my eyes and just begged God to help us.

With every tilt, lurch, and bump, my breathing became a little more shallow. I moved over to the window seat and stared down below us, trying to guess how far the ground really was.

Too far.

And it was all ocean. The dark water stretched as far as I could see. It looked choppy and churned as if there was also a storm raging beneath the surface of the sea.

Even if we survived the plane crashing, the chances of not drowning were slim. I wasn't sure which way I would prefer to die. Thinking about it made me feel extremely sick. It was like asking a person if they wanted to be shot or stabbed. The answer was neither.

The answer was I didn't want to die.

A gust of wind attacked the plane, tossing it up into the air and turning us onto our side. I finally understood the reason for the seatbelt because had I not been wearing it, I would have fallen across the plane and hit the other side.

I sucked in a deep breath. I couldn't scream. I was beyond screaming. I was so utterly terrified that my body just hung there like a ragdoll and trembled. When the plane righted, my body jerked in the seat, my head bouncing off the window.

And then we fell out of the sky.

The plane literally took a nosedive toward the ocean.

I no longer had to wonder if this plane had the oxygen masks built into the ceiling because they fell out, one of them dangling in front of me. I stared at it, numb, knowing I needed to put it on but unable to command my body to move.

Nash appeared, his face pale and his light-green eyes wild. He stumbled over to me and my eyes snapped up. "Who's driving the plane!" I demanded, already knowing no one was.

He didn't say anything. He just strapped the mask over my face and then turned to go back to the cockpit. I grabbed his hand as oxygen made its way into my lungs.

Our eyes met.

His fingers tightened around mine.

It was the kind of moment that needed no words. We both knew exactly what was happening. We barely knew each other. We were only connected through our family ties, and now it seemed we might die together.

His face would be the last one I would see.

His skin would be the last skin I felt.

Both our lives would be cut short and we would be left with nothing but a bunch of what ifs.

"I'm going to do everything I can to keep us alive," he vowed.

I clung to his words after he disappeared. I replayed them over and over in my head. It wasn't a promise. It wasn't a guarantee.

It was all I had.

A clap of thunder boomed through the sky and caused me to jump about a mile high in my seat. It was so close and so loud it shook the plane. The hum of the engine sputtered. I heard Nash radioing for help. I heard him begging for someone to answer. No one did.

The tiny plane plummeted, quickly losing altitude, barreling toward the ocean as the storm raged around us. I unhooked my seatbelt, tore the mask from my face, and went for Nash. If I was going to die, I wasn't going to be alone.

He barely glanced at me when I sat in the seat beside him. He was pulling on the controls, sweat dotting his forehead and trailing down his face. As soon as he would manage to get the nose of the plane pulled back up, it would only force itself back down again. It was a vicious cycle—up and down, up and down.

As the body of water drew closer, I began to brace myself for impact. I knew the force and speed we were traveling would slam us into the water like it was a wall of concrete. There wasn't anything left to do.

With a loud curse, Nash let go of the controls. He turned to me. We shared another of those meaningful looks, and then he was leaping over the controls separating us and covering my body with his.

He was trying to protect me.

Tears leaked out of my eyes and fell onto the cold, hard floor of the plane.

Nash started speaking softly to me. In Spanish. The cadence of his words was like a song. I didn't bother to ask him what he was saying. I didn't care.

I was just glad the last sound I would ever hear was his beautiful voice.

The plane screamed on impact, buckling under the pressure of whatever we hit and groaned with such ferocity that any hope we would survive vanished.

And then there was nothing.

Cambria Hebert

THE ISLAND...

3

It could have been hours. It could have been days. I didn't know how long we floated between the living and the dead. All I knew was that time had passed. The peaceful sound of the waves crashing along a sand-filled shore was the first thing I heard when my ears came alive.

The sound was soothing and I snuggled down in my bed, trying to get comfortable.

But there was no comfort.

One of my eyes opened and all I could see was chaos. Debris littered the area around me. Something poked into my side and my body began to tingle. As my mind cleared of its self-imposed fog, I became aware of the stiffness in my muscles, the pain lingering in my limbs, and of a searing, slicing pain radiating throughout in my skull.

Plane crash.
Dead.
No... Alive.
Nash.

The final thought caused me to push up off the floor quickly. Too quickly, because I fell right back down into a pathetic heap. Refusing to accept the way I felt, I pushed up again, this time a little bit slower. I blinked, squinting through the dimness of the interior of the plane.

Or what was left of it.

The entire tail section was gone.

And beyond it...

Beyond were dense leafy greenery and the chatter of foreign-sounding birds. But I wasn't ready to think about where we might be or what might lie in wait tucked deep inside the foliage. My first concern was for the man who tried to protect me even when we were falling from the sky.

He was no longer on top of me.

He was no longer beside me.

I didn't see him at all. Suddenly an all-encompassing panic gripped me like a vise. What if he was sucked out the back half of the plane? What if he was out there injured or... worse?

Calm down, Ava! I demanded of myself. *He didn't fall out of the plane. He was right here, with you. If he had fallen out, you would have too.*

Thank goodness there was some voice of reason left inside me.

I sat up, pushing away some of the debris— pieces of the plane, papers, glass—and peering into what was left of the back section of the plane. Some of the seats were missing. Some had come loose and were lying on their sides. Oxygen masks still dangled from what was left of the ceiling, some knotted together, some missing parts. A couple of the windows were busted out, allowing in a little bit of light.

I walked carefully through the area, balancing my hand on the walls as I walked. Over toward the left, underneath a few windows, was a pile of three chairs. Sticking out from beneath them was a foot.

I lunged forward, tripping a little and falling into the chair on the top. I grabbed it and hauled it backward. My muscles strained under the weight, but I kept at it. When it was gone, I was able to see more of Nash's still body.

"Nash," I said, my voice sounding like a rusty saw scraping across metal. "Wake up. Please don't be dead."

My vision was blurry from the tears soaking my eyes, but I kept working, shoving back another chair and uncovering his face. I dropped to my knees beside him and took his jaw in my hands. I tilted his head toward me and put my ear right up to his lips.

He was breathing.

He looked so vulnerable lying there with blood smeared across his cheek and dark curls falling over his forehead. I reached out and brushed them away, revealing a bruise on his forehead. "Nash," I said again, his name more of a whispered prayer.

His eyelashes fluttered. He groaned. And then he was staring up at me, disoriented and confused.

"The plane crashed. We're still alive. We're okay."

I watched realization dawn over his features. I watched him go through the mental body check I'd just performed on myself. And then he was springing up at impossible speed, startling me, and I fell back.

But he caught me.

He pulled me into his chest, crushing me against him. Rocking us back and forth while he palmed the back of my head. I held on to him as tightly as I could, ignoring the protest in my joints, the tremor of my hands.

We were both alive. *Thank you, God.*

His body stiffened and he pulled me back, his eyes searching my face. "Are you hurt? How badly are you injured?"

"I'm not sure. What about you?"

"I think I'm okay. Nothing too serious."

"You're bleeding," I said softly, reaching up to touch the red smeared on his cheek.

"So are you," he murmured, grasping my head and tilting it down. "You have a gash in your head. It looks pretty deep, but I can't be sure because it's caked with dried blood and your hair."

"That explains the headache," I joked, though it wasn't funny.

"We need to get up, move around, and really find out how badly we're injured."

I nodded.

Gently, he sat me away from him and stood. He reached down and helped me to my feet and then linked our fingers. "We stay together."

I nodded again.

He moved back toward the cockpit and started digging through the rubble. When the plane's radio came into sight, a shaky sigh escaped my lips. That radio was our lifeline. That radio was our ticket to getting help. I watched Nash as he flipped the switches, as he used the controls and held the little microphone at his lips.

"Mayday, Mayday," he said into the radio.

Silence followed.

Nash fiddled with the switches some more. He shook the radio and cursed at it impolitely.

Still, the electronic was unresponsive.

"Shit!" Nash said, kicking it to the side. He pushed his hand through the tangled mass of curls on his head and growled. "It's broken."

Well, yeah, I kind of figured that when he kicked it.

The sharp swell of disappointment was strong. So was the fear. Would anyone know where to look for us? How long until someone noticed we never landed? I pressed a hand to my head gingerly. All this worrying and thinking only made it hurt worse.

I caught Nash looking at me with a heavy frown on his face. I gave him what I hoped was an encouraging smile and released my head. He waded through the mess, moving things out of this way, until he reached a little cabinet built into the wall of the plane. Using the side of his fist, Nash hit the little cabinet door and it sprang open. A large white first aid kit spilled out.

"Sweet," he said, scooping it up. He scrounged around a few more minutes and came up with two bottles of water. Just looking at them made me realize how thirsty I was.

He uncapped one of the bottles and extended it to me. I took it, lifting the lukewarm liquid to my lips. It slid across my tongue and down my throat with ease, rinsing away some of the dryness. A small sound of appreciation ripped from my chest, and I greedily took another gulping sip.

I caught Nash watching me from over the bottle still stuck to my lips. I stopped drinking immediately and held it out to him. I felt selfish just then, hogging down the water when he likely was just as thirsty as I.

He gave me a small shake of his head and held up the other bottle. "That one is yours."

I watched as he uncapped his own bottle and took a drink. My gaze fastened right to his throat when his Adam's apple bobbed up and down with every swallow. He had another smear of blood on his neck and some splotches of dirt. My fingers itched to reach out and brush it away, to feel for his steady pulse at the base of his neck. The need to touch him—to reassure myself that we were indeed alive and breathing—was almost overwhelming.

I pulled the bottle away from my lips, my thirst satiated but an all-new need arising within in.

He seemed to sense the change in the air around us and he too lowered the bottle from his lips and recapped it. Keeping his green-eyed stare on me, he reached out and took my bottle, twisting the cap back onto it as well.

"We need to drink slowly, try and save this until we know what we're dealing with."

I saw his lips move. I heard the deep timbre of his voice. But I barely heard his words. I stepped forward and wrapped my arms around his waist, bringing myself tightly up against him. I rested my ear over his chest, just like I had craved to do, and pressed it there, seeking out the sound I so badly needed.

He gave it to me without even trying. The rhythm of his heart echoed through his chest and filled me up. My eyes slid closed as I stood there, wrapped around him, listening to the proof that we had survived, that we really were alive.

One of his arms came up, hovered over my back, and then descended, wrapping around me with strength and purpose. He took a deep breath and my ear rose with his chest, his heartbeat getting just a little bit closer.

"I really thought we were going to die." I confessed.

"I'd be lying if I said I didn't think that too."

He hugged me just a little bit tighter and I felt his cheek press against the top of my head. I winced, sharp pain cutting into our moment.

"I need to look at you," he murmured, pulling away gently.

He handed me the first-aid kit and then grabbed one of the fallen plane seats and righted it, motioning for me to come and sit down. I did and he stood over me, his fingers gently probing my head.

"You have a piece of shrapnel stuck in your head," he muttered.

He continued to search around for a moment and then squatted down before me, turning the kit in my lap and then clicking it open and rummaging through its contents. He came out with a pair of tweezers, and I cringed.

"I'll be gentle," he promised.

I figured the pain couldn't be any worse than falling from the sky in a plane so I nodded and gave him full access to my wound. It didn't take him long to pull out the scrap of metal, my teeth grinding together as he did. It stung. It felt like it was a mile long, and I sensed every single inch as he yanked.

"Hold out your hand," he said, and when I did he dropped a fairly sizeable piece of the plane into my palm. It was smeared with rust-colored blood and was probably two inches in length.

Then he abandoned the tweezers and quickly reached for a thick wad of gauze, pressing into my scalp. "You're bleeding again," he said grimly.

I didn't say anything because there wasn't anything I could say that would make the blood stop flowing.

"Hold this," he instructed, and I reached up to apply pressure to the wound. I could feel the warm liquid already soaking through the gauze to coat my fingers. Vaguely, I wondered how much blood I already lost, how much more blood I could afford to lose.

Nash was searching through the first aid kit, which thank goodness was a good size and stocked full. He lined up a few items on the top of the pile and then looked up.

"Do you trust me?"

"Yes." How could I not trust a man who tried to save us and when it became obvious he couldn't, he still covered my body with his?

"I'm going to clean your wound and then stitch it closed. It's going to hurt. I'm sorry."

The bottom dropped out of my stomach. "Have you ever stitched up someone's head?"

"You're my first."

"Words every girl longs to hear," I quipped.

He grinned. It made me forget for just a moment that I was bleeding profusely from my scalp.

"We gotta get this bleeding stopped," he said gently, reaching up and pulling away my hand. The gauze came with it. It was completely soaked in red.

"Don't look at it," he said, tossing it aside and ripping open some kind of wipe or something. He swiped it across my head and I gave a shout of pain.

"Shit!" I yelled. "That hurts."

"I like it when women talk dirty to me," he said, continuing the torture.

"I'll just bet you do," I muttered darkly.

He chuckled and reached for another wipe. My heart pounded and my vision became a little blurry.

"You're doing good," he would say every few minutes.

Then he reached for a needle and some black thread. I thought I might pass out. I started shaking uncontrollably, my teeth chattering together like we were sitting in an igloo in shorts and T-shirts.

"Ava," he said. He sounded so far away.

Then his warm hands were gripping my chin and he was turning my face up so he could stare down into my eyes. "Don't you dare pass out on me."

I just kept shaking. He cursed.

And then he climbed into my lap.

That was one way to get a girl's attention.

His weight settled over me like a heavy blanket. His warmth was like a sauna and my skin soaked him in like a blooming flower on the first day of spring. His thighs were huge and they rested on each side of my waist, the core of him meeting my middle and his body pinning me back against the seat.

"You're going into shock," he explained. "Just breathe."

I thought his weight might seem crushing, but it wasn't. It was security; it was something solid in a tentative world. My hands twisted in the hem of his shirt and held on, their shaking slowing to a fine tremble.

"That's a girl," he murmured, placing his lips against my forehead.

My body calmed. My heart rate returned to normal. What he did for me nothing in that first aid kit could do.

"I'm going to go as fast as I can," he promised.

I wondered what he was talking about.

And then the needled jabbed into my skin. I yelped and he bore his weight down on me even further, pinning me to the chair and keeping me still.

I hoped I never had to feel this kind of pain again. I felt every jab, every pull of the needle. It hurt so bad I sort of went numb. It was as if my body refused to feel that amount of pain.

And then he pulled his hands away.

I collapsed against the back of the chair like I'd just completed a marathon.

"Hey," he murmured softly, taking my face in his hands. "You still with me?"

I nodded.

He kissed me.

The first brush of his lips was balm to my pain-laden soul. It was a soft, lingering kiss that stole my senses and made everything, including the pain, disappear. He titled his head just slightly, his lips dragging over mine. Mine parted and our mouths met again. His tongue teased the entrance of my mouth, tracing the outline of my lips, and then he planted his lips fully upon mine once more.

It was the best pain medicine I would ever know.

A small whimper left my mouth and traveled into his. He swallowed it like he was trying to capture some of my pain and take it away, like he was willing to shoulder some of my hurt so I would know relief.

It wasn't really about romance. It wasn't about passion.

It was more.

When he pulled back, he dropped a soft kiss to the tip of my nose. "*Bella*," he whispered, the word sounding poetic as he spoke it in his native language.

It was probably the only word I knew in Spanish. It meant "beautiful."

"I'm going to cover this now," he said gently, reaching down beside us, cleaning off his hands and then rummaging around for more supplies out of the kit. "The worst of the pain is over."

His kiss lingered on my lips. The taste of him clung to the inside of my mouth while he finished cleaning the area around my new stitches and then applied some sort of covering.

"There," he said, climbing off my lap. I instantly missed his weight. "That's the best I could do considering all this hair." He reached out and fingered a thick lock of my wavy, long blond hair.

"Thank you." I looked up. Noticing the blood and gash on his cheek once more. "Your turn."

I motioned for him to take my seat and I crouched, searching around for some supplies of my own to clean his injury. I lined them up on his lap, kneeled between his knees, and leaned into him to clean off the area.

The muscle in his jaw ticked as I cleaned off the worst of the area. It wasn't still bleeding so I figured a butterfly bandage would do just fine. I tried not to be distracted by the way his hand found the side of my hip and held on to me while I worked.

Who was I kidding?

It was distracting as hell.

I guess my libido didn't get damaged in the crash.

After I applied the antiseptic and bandage, I pulled back. "I think you'll live," I declared.

"That's good. I'm not ready to die yet."

I swallowed. Was there a veiled meaning behind his words? I could have sworn desire laced his eyes. I told myself I was just seeing things because of my discomfort.

A sound from outside caught my attention. I stood up abruptly. "Where are we?" I murmured, nervous about what lay beyond the wreckage.

"Don't know. Probably one of the many islands around here."

"We should find a hospital. Or the police."

He gave me a long glance out of the corner of his eye but didn't say anything. Even still, that one glance made me uneasy.

"Come on," he said, packing up the first aid kit and tucking it beneath his arm with one of the water bottles. I grabbed up mine and he took my hand, leading us to the back of the plane.

"Stay here," he said and then hopped down over the jagged metal and loose wiring into the jungle-like environment. He glanced out into the foliage and then back at me.

I could see his internal debate about whether or not to leave me or drag me along with him. Too bad it wasn't his decision.

"Stay together." I reminded him of his earlier words.

He nodded and palmed my waist, lifting me down as if I weighed nothing at all. When he sat me on my feet, he reached up and brushed away the hair that was sticking to my forehead in what I assumed was dried blood.

It appeared the plane crashed onto the shore and skidded into a densely wooded area. I figured we couldn't have hit the ocean because nothing inside the plane was wet, and surely some of the salty seawater would have made it inside with the busted windows and half the plane missing. What was left of the plane rested among palm trees and plants with leaves as big as my head. Behind it, the earth bore the skid marks of its hasty crash and it was those marks we followed, kind of like Hansel and Gretel followed the breadcrumbs.

It didn't take long to see where they led. It wasn't to a cottage made of candy. It was to a pristine stretch of beach.

The sand was white, the water a crystal-clear blue. In the distance, the sun was sinking low in the sky, painting the horizon shades of pink and orange, setting a blazing trail of crimson along the top of the water.

It was absolutely stunning.

Except for one thing.

There wasn't a single soul in sight. There were no boats. No people. No hotels, no streets, no noise. It was as if this place had been previously untouched by any kind of civilization.

I glanced at Nash and the solemn set to his jaw. I finally understood the look he'd given me on the plane when I talked about a hospital and the police.

There would be no hospital. Or police. There would be no help at all.

It appeared that Nash and I had crashed on an uninhabited island.

We were utterly alone.

4

We walked for a long time, thinking we would run into some kind of civilization, not yet willing to give up hope. But every step we took only got us closer to the realization that there was no one here but us.

We were on an island. A tropical oasis of nothing but sand, water, and lush tropical growth. The sand was white and the water was crystal clear. The beach stretched on for as far as I could see and the sand gave way to a jungle of sorts. We didn't really explore too deeply into the foliage. I was afraid of getting lost. And we were both exhausted.

We might have been out for some time, but it hadn't been a restful sleep. It had been our bodies' way of healing, of keeping us both alive.

When it became apparent that there was nothing out there and darkness threatened to consume all the light of day that remained, we turned back, heading for the plane. My stomach rumbled as we walked and I struggled to remember the last time I ate. I glanced at Nash, who had fallen quiet. His jeans were rolled up above his knees, one falling slightly lower than the other. He walked in the water as it rushed up over his feet and ankles. A breeze blew off the ocean, pulling at his T-shirt, plastering it against his torso, which was clearly well defined.

He must've felt my stare because he looked up.

"When we get back to the plane, I will try to radio for help. Maybe we'll get lucky and have a signal."

I nodded. "Maybe we can find one of our phones."

"I think staying near the plane is our best bet right now. If someone comes looking, they might spot the wreckage."

"And the plane is good shelter," I added. Even if the tail end was missing, it still provided a barrier from the elements and the sun. Not to mention we really had no idea what kind of predators lived on the island.

"Do you think we're close to Puerto Rico?" I asked him.

"I couldn't say. The plane was blown farther out into the sea… If I had to guess, I would say we're closer to Bermuda."

We crashed in the Bermuda Triangle?

He nodded, his expression grim.

I wasn't sure what this could mean. Sure, I'd heard all the tales and rumors about the triangle and how planes and boats often went missing. Were we just another victim of the esteemed black hole of the ocean? Were we going to fade into something of a mystery? Would we fall victim to a myth?

I pushed those thoughts away, telling myself it didn't matter. The only thing that mattered right now was that we were alive.

The plane came into view in the distance, an all too vivid reminder of what we just endured. Both of us trudged on, me wishing I had some kind of pain medicine to dull the throbbing in my head and Nash saying nothing at all.

It was completely dark when we made our way inside the wreckage. I was exhausted and felt like crying. We both plopped down in two wayward chairs. Nash was nothing but a blur of color in the darkness.

"Let's just rest tonight. We'll figure out what we're going to do in the morning."

"Good idea."

He stood and pried open the overhead compartments above the row of seats. He pulled something down, shaking it out and then draping the blanket over me. Then he handed me a pillow.

"What about you?"

"I'll get one for me too."

I snuggled down into the seat with my blanket and pillow, telling myself things could be far, far worse. And then I closed my eyes. My thoughts drifted to Nash and the way I felt earlier when his lips were upon mine.

*   *   *

Sleep was rather easy to obtain… but it was hard to keep. I kept hearing the crunch of metal, the sound of the tail being ripped away. And then I would somehow break free of the pile of debris burying me and stand, wind whipping around me evilly, trying to pull me from the plane. And then I would see him. See Nash. He would reach for me and I would hold out my hand…

And then the wind would claim him, would suck him right into the darkened sky outside.

His scream rang through my head.

I jerked awake.

"Ava?" His voice reached me through the dark.

"Nash." Just the sound of his voice washed away the worst of the dream.

I heard some movement and then he appeared above me. "Did you have a nightmare?"

I nodded and realized that he likely couldn't see the movement. "Yeah. I'm okay now."

"Wanna talk about it?"

"The plane was crashing all over again. But this time… you didn't make it." I couldn't help the way my voice caught at the last part.

He made a soft sound and reached for me, picking me up and sitting down with me in his lap. My skin felt cold against his and I sighed at his warmth enveloping me.

"Where the hell is your blanket?" he asked, feeling around the ground around us. He found it and dragged it up, tucking it around us both.

"I must have kicked it off when I was sleeping."

He grunted. "Those shorts of yours aren't going to keep you warm."

"What's wrong with my shorts?"

"Not a thing," he said, his voice a little thicker than before. "They just don't offer much warmth."

They *were* short. And I *was* cold.

"Like your jeans are any warmer." I snorted, reaching down and fingering one of the many holes. My fingertip slid in and brushed against the skin of his leg. Heat fizzled along my nerve endings, zapping up my fingers through my arm and toward my chest. I jerked back, a little frightened about the sudden surge of desire.

He chuckled.

I felt my muscles stiffen slightly, a little shocked at my response from an accidental touch.

He seemed to sense the change that came over me, and his hand slid upward and rubbed slow circles over my back, coaxing my body into relaxing once more. It worked. My eyes closed and I submitted to the feel of his palm massaging me.

I snuggled a little closer, not even realizing what I was doing until his arms tightened around me. I might have been embarrassed about my body's automatic reaction to get closer if he hadn't felt so damn good. I'd never been held like this before. Sure, I'd seen women and men on TV embracing and oh-so-close, but I didn't really think it would feel this way. This secure.

Maybe it was that sense of security that caused the one secret fear that had been gnawing at me since we crashed to pass through my lips.

"Do you think anyone will come for us?" I whispered. The words were captured by the darkness around us, creeping in the empty space, almost taunting us.

He was silent a moment and then he replied. "Yes. I really do. We're going to be just fine." His lips grazed the top of my forehead as he spoke. Hot chills raced over my skin.

I desperately wanted to believe him. Still, there was a taunting voice inside me that whispered we would never get off this island.

I spent the rest of the night in that place between sleep and consciousness. Usually that state annoyed me because it wasn't actually restful, but this time I wasn't annoyed. I was so comfortable it was like I didn't quite want to surrender to sleep, because then I wouldn't be aware of his breathing, of the steady rhythm of his heart. I wouldn't feel the way his skin brushed against mine when he moved.

The darkness started to lift, bringing out more shadows, and I became aware of needs that required the bathroom we didn't have. I felt myself squirm in his lap, knowing I couldn't hold it forever, but not wanting to use the jungle out there as a potty.

He groaned a little, his hips bucking up, pressing a very solid length against my hip. I froze. Squirming around in a guy's lap probably wasn't the best idea. He moved again, the hard length of him nudging me.

My mouth went dry.

I wasn't really sure how to react. Part of me wanted to leap off him. The other part of me was curious. My fingers itched to reach out and explore that part of him—the part of a man that was sort of a mystery to me.

Before I could do anything, he opened his eyes and I felt his stare. A half smile played across his lips. "Good morning."

"Hi," I said shyly.

"It's still really early."

"I have to pee," I said, totally embarrassed I just announced that like a five-year-old, but clearly the feel of his... well, his *you know*, robbed my brain of the filter it obviously needed.

He chuckled. "Yeah, me too." He patted my back. "Come on, then, up."

I swung my legs off him, which pressed my bottom farther back in his lap. A groan ripped out of his throat as the ridge in his pants punched forward, right up against my backside.

I froze, not really sure what to do. I hoped he didn't think I did that on purpose.

"He's not going to get any smaller with you sitting in my lap like that," he murmured.

Embarrassment flooded my cheeks and I jolted off him, stumbling a little over the debris on the ground. Nash grabbed my arm to steady me but didn't say anything else, thank God.

We went outside and he pointed to the right. "Ladies that way." Then he started off to the left.

I wandered around a few minutes, squinting at every shape I saw, half expecting some kind of wild beast to attack me and make me breakfast. When nothing came after me, I found a spot and did my business, the whole time wrinkling my nose. I was so not a roughing it kind of girl.

Nash was waiting beside the plane when I pushed my way back through the plants. His back was to me and he was staring out toward the beach. He didn't turn, but he held out his hand to me. "Look," he said, his voice hushed.

I stepped forward, slipping my hand into his, and gasped.

The sun was rising over the ocean. The sky was a vibrant hue of pink with the pale yellow of the sun in the center. The water sparkled like a chest full of gems and a light, cool breeze brushed over my skin and ruffled the large leaves around us.

"I've never seen a sunrise so beautiful."

"It's the ultimate love story," he murmured.

"What?" I glanced away from the view to his strong profile. I couldn't help but study the planes and angles of his face and the slight stubble that covered the bottom portion of his jaw.

"The story about how the moon loved the sun so deeply that it died every morning so she could breathe with the new day."

I glanced back at the climbing sun. "I've never heard that before."

"Two entities intertwined forever, destined to never share the sky at the same time, but never able to hate each other for it. Instead, they die for one other over and over again."

"That's beautiful." And it brought an entirely new significance to night and day.

"*Si*," he agreed.

We stood there unmoving, staring out at the water until the sun had ascended above the verge and appeared to be sitting on top of the horizon like a giant boat ready to sail away.

"Kiki would have loved to see this," I said, thinking of my beloved grandmother. Then panic stole through me and I gasped. "Kiki!"

Forgetting all about the beautiful sunrise, I raced back toward the plane—toward the last place I remembered seeing the suitcase with the urn inside.

Before the crash.

Before the tail of the plane was whipped away and Nash and I were knocked out cold.

I couldn't believe I had forgotten about her ashes until now. What if they were gone? What if they had been sucked out of the plane when the tail was torn away?

It would be like losing her all over again.

5

I searched furiously through the wreckage, my heart pounding and tears swimming in my eyes. Surely she was still here. Surely life couldn't be so cruel as to kill a woman twice.

I felt the jab of something sharp in my hand and I yelped, yanking it back and seeing blood. I wiped in on my shirt and kept on rummaging.

Nash searched alongside me, lifting up the heavier items that I didn't have the muscle to move. Dread spread through my limbs the longer we looked and came up empty. I was about to completely lose it when Nash called out from behind. "Found it!"

I made a sound of relief and rushed over as he pulled the black suitcase from underneath a pile of junk. It was scuffed up and the fabric was lightly shredded. He laid it down and I ripped at the zippers, my fingers just not being able to move fast enough. When I got it opened, I flung the lid back and stared down at the contents inside.

The urn was still in once piece. It was completely unharmed.

A single tear slid down my cheek as I lifted the container carefully, inspecting it and then hugging it close to my chest.

"Thank you," I whispered to Nash.

He wrapped me and the urn in his arms and held me close while the strongest of my emotions rolled through me. I could bear to lose anything else to this crash except for this.

He pulled back and wiped at the tear on my cheek. Then he looked at my hand and frowned. "You're bleeding."

"I'm okay."

He retrieved the first aid kit, and I scowled at him. "I've had enough stitches to last me a lifetime. If you plan on pulling anything out of that case other than a Band-Aid, I'm going to kick you."

"So violent," he said, grinning.

I narrowed my eyes.

"Will you consent to a little antibacterial cream as well?"

"Fine," I grumbled and flung out my hand.

"I think we should clean this place up a bit or we're going to keep hurting ourselves. Maybe we can find some soda or some food. And maybe we can find an extra blanket or two to hang up over the part that's missing." He motioned toward the gaping hole that used to be the tail.

"I have some protein bars in my suitcase if we can find it."

He nodded. "I'll try to radio for help."

As promised, he applied a Band-Aid and then put away the kit. We worked together, cleaning up the debris, lining up a few of the stray seats against the wall and blocking the broken windows with whatever we could find.

My eyes strayed to the broken radio. Regret burned the back of my throat. How different things would've been if we could just call someone. But there would be no calling for help.

But I did manage to find my suitcase, and I squealed with joy. I had a toothbrush, a comb, and even some tiny bottles of shampoo and soap! I'd never been so excited over shampoo.

Nash managed to find three cans of soda, another water bottle, and a couple bags of peanuts and pretzels and piled them in an extra chair. I added the box of Luna bars to the stash and the pack of gum I found in my suitcase. It wasn't much, but it was a hell of a lot better than nothing.

By the time we were done, I was sweaty, thirsty, and even dirtier.

"I have some bad news," Nash said, coming out of the cockpit and looking at me grimly.

"What?" I asked, a sinking feeling in my stomach.

He held up a cell phone. A very broken and cracked cell phone.

"Was that yours?"

He nodded. "It's useless."

"I haven't even found mine."

"I didn't find another either."

The odds of one of our cells even getting any service here, if they worked, was slim to none anyway, so I tried not to take it too hard.

"I found the protein bars," I said, holding up the box, trying to lighten the mood.

"God, I'm starving."

He took the box out of my hands and looked at it. Then he looked back at me and lifted an eyebrow. "Nutrition for women?" he read off the front.

I grinned. "Don't worry. If you start to grow boobs, I'll lend you a bra."

He gave me a wolfish smile. "Does that mean you wouldn't be wearing one?"

Desire swirled low in my belly and for a few long moments, I stared at him, unable to say a word. Then I snapped out of it. "I found my suitcase," I said dumbly. "I have extra."

"Too bad," he drawled, looking back at the box. "So why are these for women?"

I shrugged. "I think it's because they're high in folic acid and vitamin D. Those are vitamins that are especially good for women."

"Chocolate chip cookie dough flavored," he said. "I'll eat anything flavored like a cookie, even if I start to grow boobs."

I laughed. "They're my favorite."

"What do you say we take our dinner and only meal today out on the beach?"

I nodded. He opened the box and pulled out two bars with brown and blue wrappers and the words *Luna Protein* scrawled across the front. "These are tiny," he grumped.

"They fill me up." I defended my snacks.

He snorted. "You're tiny too."

"I'm almost five-foot-seven!"

"I'm six-three."

"Take two," I lamented, realizing a single bar definitely wasn't going to be enough for him.

[53]

He shook his head. "No way. We have to conserve this stuff."

I nodded. He grabbed up a can of Coke and motioned for me to follow him. We made our way down to the sand in no time. The sun was still pretty high in the sky so I knew we had hours of daylight left.

We sat down side by side, facing the ocean, and he handed me a bar. I tore open the wrapper, relieved to see only a little bit of the chocolate coating had melted onto the inside of the wrapper. I groaned when the chocolate hit my tongue. "So good," I moaned.

"If you could eat anything in the world right now, what would it be?" Nash asked me as he took a big bite of his bar.

"Hmmm. Veggie pizza with the pan crust from Pizza Hut. That's the thickest. And a chocolate milkshake."

"A girl that knows what she wants."

"What about you?"

"A huge cheeseburger piled high with all the fixings, onion rings, and a chocolate Coke."

"A chocolate Coke?"

"Please tell me you've had it," he said, stuffing the final bite of his dinner in his mouth.

"Never even heard of it."

He fell back on the sand like he'd been shot.

I giggled. "What is it?"

"It's basically a fountain Coke with chocolate syrup swirled in it."

"That doesn't sound like it goes together," I said, wrinkling my nose.

"Silence, woman!" he commanded. Then he gave me an ornery smile.

I rolled my eyes and took another bite of my bar and suddenly felt guilty for eating it. His was gone and I knew he had to be starving.

"Open your mouth and close your eyes, and you will get a big surprise," I repeated the rhyme from my childhood.

"Do you have a dead bug in your pocket or something?"

I wagged my eyebrows. "Are you scared?"

Challenge flared in his eyes and then he closed them and opened his mouth. I popped the rest of my uneaten bar into his waiting mouth. When his lips closed around it his eyes shot open and he sat up. He didn't chew, just stared at me. "What the hell did you do that for?" he said around the mouthful of food.

"You shouldn't talk with food in your mouth," I informed him.

He gave me a dark look.

"You need it more than I do. I'm fine." In truth, I was starving too, but I was smaller and didn't need as much as him.

He acted like he was going to spit it out into his hand. I grabbed his very impressive bicep. "Don't you dare," I warned. "That's a waste of perfectly good food."

He made a frustrated sound and then gave in and chewed it up. "Why did you do that!" he demanded when he was done.

I tilted my head to the side. "Because you saved my life."

He snorted. "Honey, I crashed the plane."

I shook my head. "I'm pretty sure you're the only reason it landed here instead of diving straight into the ocean and killing us both."

"I didn't do enough. I didn't keep it up in the air."

I reached out and covered my hand with his. He looked at our hands and then back at me. "When you realized we were going down, that it couldn't be stopped, do you remember what you did?"

"Tried not to shit my pants?" he guessed.

I smiled. "Well, thank goodness you didn't. Then I'd be stuck smelling you."

He snorted.

I turned serious again. "You covered my body with yours." For some reason, that replayed over and over in my head—the weight of him pressing me down. The sound of his foreign tongue whispering to me softly... Maybe it hadn't meant anything. Maybe it was just a kneejerk reaction on his part, but to me... to me it meant more than he would ever know. That moment was branded into my brain and my heart forever.

"It was the only thing I could think of," he said, not brushing off what I said. Something in my chest swelled just a little when those green eyes met mine. "I didn't know any other way to keep you alive."

"Even if it meant you getting hurt," I whispered.

How had we gotten so close? Our noses were almost touching. I could feel his warm, chocolate-scented breath across my face. In that moment, I forgot we were stranded. I forgot I was filthy. That my head hurt and that we might never make it home. In that second when his gaze touched mine, we were just two people who were irrevocably drawn to each other. Two people sitting in a tropical paradise with the sound of the waves echoing around us and the hum of chemistry between us.

He swallowed; I heard his saliva slide down his throat. "I didn't do a very good job," he said low.

The huskiness in his voice almost overshadowed his words. Almost.

"What do you mean?"

He reached out tentatively and touched around the tender area where my stitches were. "You're still the one that got hurt the most."

"But you fixed me up."

The corner of his mouth turned up.

He was going to kiss me.

I felt the pull between us so strongly that it took my breath.

He trailed his fingers down from my head, across my cheek, and then traced the line beneath my bottom lip. Then he cleared his throat and pulled away.

I blinked rapidly, shocked that he hadn't followed through. My body screamed for him to come back.

"You need to drink this," he said, his voice still husky. I knew he had to be as affected by me as I was by him. Or was that only wishful thinking? "The sugar will do you good."

"Only if you drink some too."

He nodded and popped the top on the can.

Brown, fizzy liquid sprayed up, making me squeal and lurch away. I looked back at Nash, who was still holding the can out away from him, with droplets of the sugary soda all over his arms and face.

I pressed a hand over my lips, trying to stop the giggle.

He glanced at me. A drop of soda dripped off his nose and he caught it with his tongue. I lost it. I laughed so hard I fell over in the sand.

"You think that's funny, huh?" he said, not amused at all.

He turned away and my giggles died away. "I'm sorry," I said, sitting up, reaching out for his shoulder.

He pounced on me. Literally turned and tackled me into the sand. Pinning me to the ground, he shook his head, his dark curls flinging droplets of soda onto my face. I squealed.

"Not so funny now, is it?" he said, rubbing his damp cheek across mine.

His lips brushed the corner of my mouth.

I froze, no longer able to laugh.

My stomach dropped and then started to dance around. He was literally on top of me, his body pressed along mine. Just the mere tease of his lips was enough to make my hands tremble and my knees weak.

He pulled back just a fraction of an inch, turned his head, and stared down at me. I could barely read his expression because of the way the sun shone around his body like a halo, making him look like he was in the shadows.

But I didn't need to see his expression.

Because something was pressing against my stomach. Something hard and urgent. Something that I had to make an effort not to wiggle against.

His mouth claimed mine. He literally stole every feeling I was experiencing and replaced them with only him. His kiss was so utterly consuming, so all-encompassing, that I could do nothing but allow him to ravage my mouth, again and again.

Oh my God, it was the single most devastating experience of my life. He was truly delicious. He tasted like chocolate and salt. His body was hard and lean. Our toes twirled around together in the sand, the grittiness teasing my skin as his tongue tantalized my mouth.

"Open for me," he murmured against my lips.

I obeyed without thinking and his tongue swept inside my mouth, caressing over my teeth and fondling the roof of my mouth. He sucked my lower lip into his mouth and moved against me. I cried out because the sensation of his body and his mouth at the same time was almost more than I could bear.

There was a gnawing hunger inside me, and it wasn't for food. It was for something else, something I didn't quite understand. I felt like I was standing on the edge of a cliff about to tumble over and there was no parachute or net to catch me.

His jean-clad leg pushed between mine and he brought it up, the firmness of his knee right at my core. I moaned again, his body affecting mine in ways I truly didn't know was possible.

He tore his mouth from mine but kept kissing, down my neck and across my collarbone, where he nipped at the bones and made me shiver. He lifted his head, dark curls falling near his heavy-lidded eyes, and his tongue jutted out between two swollen lips, licking at the remains of our kiss.

"You taste good."

My thighs involuntarily tightened around his knee. I watched as his eyes darkened to a deep leafy green.

He brought his hands up and brushed away my hair. Some of the hair was stuck in dried blood and pulled, making me wince.

He frowned. "I should have cleaned you up."

"I'll do it."

He stood swiftly, the sea breeze brushing over my passion-fevered skin and making me wince. He reached down and grabbed my hands and pulled me to my feet. I stumbled a little, feeling dizzy, and I knew it was because of that kiss.

He kept hold of my hand and retrieved the Coke that started it all and handed it to me. "Drink."

I reached up to take it, but he shook his head and held the can to my lips. I watched him as he tilted it up and the warm soda traveled across my tongue. I drank. Then I drank some more. He was rather pushy about it, but I didn't argue. I was still drunk from that kiss.

My goodness, was he going to kiss me like that every day? If he did, I would never want to leave.

After a couple minutes, he relented, pulling the can up to his mouth. I watched his lips wrap around the aluminum as he drank. He drained the rest in seconds flat. And then we were walking back to the plane—our makeshift camp.

When we made it to the door, I glanced back over my shoulder, not remembering a single thing about the walk here.

Oh crap.

I was in trouble.

6

Inside, I went right for my suitcase, pulling out another pair of shorts and T-shirt. Instead of panties and a bra, I opted for my bikini to wear beneath my clothes. Then I fished out my little kit containing my shampoo and soap. I bundled all the items into my arms and turned.

Nash was standing in the entrance of the cockpit, watching me. In his hand he gripped a small duffle bag.

"What's that?"

"A bag that I usually keep on the plane. It has a spare change of clothes and some toiletries."

I felt my brow wrinkle. "Did you stay in Miami?"

"Not this trip, but sometimes I make stops or have layovers and it's nice to have some stuff in case I need it."

"I'm glad you found it."

He nodded. "Ready?"

We went back toward the beach. Bathing in salty ocean water wasn't the most ideal situation, but it was better than being coated in dried blood and sweat.

I stopped at the shore, looking around for a little bit of privacy. There really wasn't much. "You stay here. I'll go a little farther down," he offered.

I laid my stuff on the sand, getting out the soap and shampoo I needed as he walked away. I waited until he was still visible but far enough down and unpacking his own stuff before I started removing my clothes. I stayed in my bra and panties and waded into the water to my knees. I washed as best as I could with the lavender-scented soap while trying not to use too much. Even though it was the ocean, it still felt good to be clean. Once I felt fresher, I returned the soap to shore and grabbed up my T-shirt, which was stained with blood, and the shampoo.

I couldn't get the top of my head wet because of the stitches so I just dunked the ends of my hair and the back of my head in the water and then lathered up the bottom portion with suds. While that soaked in, I used my T-shirt as a washcloth and gingerly cleaned my face, trying to get all the dried blood and grime off my skin.

Once I was finished, I waded in a little farther and took off my panties, using a little of the shampoo to wash them in the water.

I couldn't help but be distracted by the way the water felt brushing between my legs. It was like that part of me was extra sensitive and every caress of the water made my muscles quiver with desire.

I glanced back down the beach toward Nash. He was coming up out of the ocean, water raining from his sun-kissed skin. It slid over his body like a lover, and I watched it travel down over his hips...

He was naked.

Stark ass naked.

The water brushed against me again and I groaned, the sensation making me squirm. Without thinking, I reached between my thighs, almost like my touch could stop my body from wanting something. My fingers met with moisture. Moisture that was not ocean water. This moisture was silkier and a little thicker.

I yanked my hand away.

What was wrong with me?

I couldn't possibly be wanting him. Not *that way*. After all, my body didn't work the way other women's bodies did.

I glanced back at him again, catching the side of his bare backside. Okay, so I looked longer than just a glance. But then I looked away (because he bent to pick up some clothes) and finished washing.

When he was almost dressed, I hurried out of the water, using my shirt as sort of a wrap, and dashed to my clothes. I realized I hadn't thought things through because my shirt would have made a really good towel—only now it was wet.

I pulled on my bathing suit, thankful it would dry quickly, and then I used the jean shorts I'd been wearing and hastily dried off most of my body. I used my hands to ring out what I could of my hair and then threw the wet shirt and shorts onto the sand. I would rinse those out in a minute.

Noting that Nash was getting closer, I pulled on the black linen shorts with a drawstring waistband and tied them loosely around my hips. I wasn't ready to put on my shirt yet because I wanted to let my hair dry a bit first.

Scooping up my comb, I got to work, tugging the tangles out of my thick blond hair. Here in this climate, I was likely a frizz ball waiting to happen. It certainly wasn't going to be straight like I usually styled it.

Nash arrived and I slid a glance at him. He wasn't wearing a shirt either. He was well defined and not quite as thin as I was expecting. He was definitely lean, but there was some bulk there too, mostly from muscle. His skin was bronzed and darkly tanned, smooth and hairless... except for a little trail of dark curly hair that started just below his navel and traveled into the tan cargo shorts that hung loosely on his hips.

It made me think of the yellow brick road—*follow the yellow brick road*—except this wasn't yellow. It was dark and led somewhere naughty and delightfully sinful.

I shivered.

"Are you cold?" Nash asked, concern lacing his tone.

"Me?" I said dumbly.

"Well... since there's no one else here," he said like it was obvious.

"No, I'm fine." I averted my gaze, embarrassed. I returned to combing my hair, thinking it was a good distraction from his body.

"Here, let me," he said, his voice suddenly much closer than just seconds ago. And then the heat that radiated off his skin touched me, wrapped around me, drew me closer. He took the comb from my slack fingers and started combing my hair.

How much of an onslaught was my body was supposed to take before I literally melted and slid into the sea?

Did he not know the effect he had over me? First he covered me with his body like he was a bodyguard and I was some royal princess, he held me all night after a nightmare, and then he kissed me… he freaking devoured half my soul with a single kiss… and now this. Now he was sliding his fingertips through my hair and massaging the base of my neck with a powerful hand.

"*Bella*," he murmured. He spoke so low and with such an accent I didn't understand what he said.

"What?" I asked, turning my head slightly toward him.

He leaned up into my ear and repeated the word again. "*Bella*. It means I think you're beautiful."

He thinks I'm beautiful.

I shivered again.

The comb paused. "I will build a fire."

"A fire?"

"*Si*, for warmth."

I let him think I was cold. Telling him I was about to jump his bones was beyond my vocabulary at the moment. Not to mention the fact I was literally stunned that I actually *did* want to jump his bones.

And all this time I thought my vagina was broken.

'Course maybe it still was. Just because I felt the stirrings of desire didn't necessarily mean my vagina was ready for a full-on sex romp.

Sex romp? What the hell was I thinking? I didn't even know what a sex romp was. *I bet he does.*

I jumped at the unexpected thought.

"Ava?" he murmured, his voice and body still entirely too close. I skittered away like a nervous filly.

"Thank you," I said, pulling my hair over my shoulder and quickly braiding the length of it. When I got to the end of the braid, I realized I didn't have anything to tie it with. I went to release it and he stopped me.

"Wait." He tore a strip off of the worn gray T-shirt he'd been wearing. He came close again, wrapping the scrap around the ends of my hair and tying it tightly into a bow. Then he stepped back to admire his craftiness.

"Thank you," I said, reaching for my T-shirt, feeling way underdressed. I couldn't help but notice the way his gaze lingered over my bare skin and on the triangles of my black bikini top.

He cleared his throat. "I'm going to go look around for wood for the bonfire."

"I'll help." I moved our belongings farther up, closer to the plane, and then started looking around for wood. I wasn't very successful, but I did manage to find a few things I thought would burn. Then I figured I would be more useful creating an area to actually burn the fire so I began to clear out a space in the pristine, white sand.

By the time I was finished, the sun was beginning to slip behind the horizon and I was covered in sand. I felt gross all over again. I dared a glance around me, noting that Nash was still nowhere in sight.

Leaving the bonfire site and the meager offerings I found to burn, I went down to the water, discarding my shorts and shirt. The water was cooler now than earlier because the sun wasn't as hot, but it was still refreshing and felt great against my overheated skin.

A fish swam by my leg and I lunged at it, thinking I would capture it and make it dinner. Of course, all I ended up with was a mouthful of salt water.

I heard a yell and looked over my shoulder at Nash. He had his hands full of wood, and as I watched him, he dumped it onto the sand and jogged forward. I stood, wondering what the alarm was about, and then he stopped and put his hands on his hips.

I made my way out of the surf and walked up the sand to where he was standing. "What's the matter?"

"I thought you had fallen," he said, his gaze sweeping over my body. My nipples hardened and I fought the urge to cross my hands over my chest.

"I was trying to catch us a fish."

He laughed. "With your bare hands?"

"At least I tried," I snapped.

He patted me on the top of the head. "Thank you."

I growled.

"Here," he said, grinning, pulling his ratty gray T-shirt out of the back pocket of his shorts. "You can use it to dry off."

"Thanks," I said, accepting it and toweling off my arms. It smelled just like him. I wondered if my skin would bear his scent after I finished drying.

"You did good clearing a space," he said and then got to work on the fire. He had the wood stacked in no time, and then I watched in fascination as he adeptly used two sticks to create a flame, which he then used some of the stuff (mostly foliage) as kindling and started what would be a very decent-sized fire.

"Where did you learn how to do that?" I asked.

"My abuelo taught me," he replied, staring at the flames. "My grandfather," he corrected. "He thought it would be good to teach me basic survival since I was going to be flying a plane."

"Looks like it came in handy."

Once the fire was in full swing, he disappeared toward the plane and I put my clothes back on. He returned with one of the plane chairs and sat it in the sand near the fire. Then he went back and got another one, sitting it right beside the first one.

It was like having a couch outside on the beach. I snickered.

"Beats getting eaten by sand fleas."

I wrinkled my nose. "You're right."

We sat down as the smoke from the bonfire wafted up into the twilight sky and created a heady, thick smell in the air around us.

We sat there for a long time, watching what was left of the sunset, while I realized that our second day on this island passed without a single trace of anyone else. Not one airplane, not one boat, nothing.

It made me wonder what our chances of being found really were.

In truth, we didn't even know where we were. We had no idea how close or far civilization could be. Suddenly, the theme song for *Gilligan's Island* was playing through my head.

"Marianne or Ginger?" I asked him.

"What?"

"You ever see reruns of *Gilligan's Island?*"

He laughed. "A couple." He turned thoughtful. "I'm partial to blondes."

Oh. Well.

Thank goodness it was getting dark because I knew I was blushing.

"What about you?" he asked after a minute.

"You want to know who I prefer?" I laughed.

He shook his head, the fire casting an orange glow over his features. "What kind of guys do you prefer?"

"I actually haven't dated in a while."

"What's a while?"

"A couple years."

He made a sound of disbelief.

"It's true," I said, shrugging. It really didn't matter if he believed me or not.

"I don't get it," he said, sitting forward and leaning his elbows on his knees. "A girl like you—"

"What's a girl like me?"

"Tall, blond hair, blue eyes, legs that go on for miles…" he said, glancing at me. "And you know you seem pretty cool too."

"Or maybe I'm just an easy target for jerks." The words came out before I could stop them. I didn't look at him for a reaction. I just stared into the flickering red and orange flames.

"If someone hasn't treated you right, he was well beyond a jerk," he said, his voice taking on a steely tone.

I didn't say anything. My past wasn't something I cared to relive. "You don't have a very thick accent for living in Puerto Rico."

He went with the change of topic, thank the stars. "I went to high school and flight school in the States. I lost my accent somewhere along the line. My father lived in the States before he married my mother."

"You went to, like, a private school?" I asked, curious.

"Yeah, my family wanted me to have a good education."

"What was it like, being away from home?"

He gave a small shrug. "At first it was hard. But they visited often and I spent all the holidays and vacations at home."

It made me wonder how wealthy his family was to afford all of that. 'Course, I didn't say it because that would be rude.

"Looking back," he continued, drawing my attention. "It was a good experience. Made me who I am today."

Something deep inside me whispered he was better than most.

I leaned back in my seat and looked up at the cobalt sky. Stars were starting to bloom above and I knew out here, away from city lights and distractions, lying under nothing but the moon and the stars would be incredible. They would spread across the sky like the ocean spread across the Atlantic.

I could hear the loud sounds of the cicadas taking over the wilderness behind us; not even the crashing waves could drown out their song. The gentle ocean breeze tugged at my hair, pulling loose strands out of the braid and whipping them against my cheek.

If I closed my eyes and didn't look at the downed plane, it would be easy to believe this was just a vacation, a getaway from life. Not essentially a prison.

"What about you?" Nash's voice interrupted my thoughts. "Did you go to college?"

"For a year." I admitted. "I hated it. My mother tried to make me keep going, telling me I couldn't do anything without a degree." I sighed. "I told her a degree wouldn't help me if I couldn't decide what I wanted the degree in. It would have been a waste of money for me to keep going and taking classes when I didn't even know if they would help me earn whatever degree I might decide on."

"I can see your point."

"I felt caged sitting in a classroom all day. I hated it. Listening to someone drone on and on about stuff they thought I should know. Who really cares what x plus y equals? No one. Who cares what the elements on the periodic table mean? I feel like there are a lot of different kinds of smart out there and not all of them come from a textbook."

"I hear some passion," he said, his tone laced with amusement.

I snorted. "That'd be the first time anyone's ever said that."

He glanced at me. "Are you serious?"

I nodded. "Back home, I'm the family member who drifts through life. The girl who doesn't finish school and who gets let go from her job. I'm the girl no one wants to date and everyone thinks is broken."

"People think you're broken?" he echoed.

Had I really just said all that? The fumes from the bonfire must have been going to my head. "Not all of me. Just certain parts."

I clamped my lips shut. Yep. The fumes were *really* getting to me.

"What parts?" he asked, his voice turning serious and a little hard.

"Forget it," I said, waving him away, trying not to die of embarrassment.

He caught my arm in a solid grip. "Tell me."

"No."

His green eyes glittered with the glow from the fire and his dark curls cast shadows across the side of his face. His jaw looked like rock-hard granite as it jutted out in anger because I refused to answer his question. His fingers tightened around me a little more and I prepared to yank away my arm.

But that's when we heard it.

An odd sort of sound.

Almost like the rhythm of drums.

Our eyes collided, both of us not daring to speak as we listened and scarcely breathed. He didn't release my wrist and I was suddenly glad because I was scared. It seemed strange to me that my first thought after realizing we may not be alone as we originally thought wasn't relief or excitement.

It was fear.

The kind of slippery fear that brushed against you like too-long grass in an empty field. The kind of fear that haunted you, that never quite went away, and you walked around feeling spooked and uneasy every second of every day. Sure, sometimes I let my head overrule my gut and I'd learned some hard lessons that way. But this time... this time my gut was screaming so loudly that I couldn't have ignored it if I tried.

The pounding of the drums continued. It was an intense and driving sound. It made my belly feel funny. And then came another sound. The sound of a loud yell or cry. I jerked and sank down in my seat.

Nash worked quickly, extinguishing the fire. We sat there for a long time, listening to the call of the drums, staring up at the starlit sky, and wondering just what in the hell was on this island with us.

I awoke grumpy and with a kink in my neck. Memories of last night pushed through my foul mood, and I realized we had far bigger problems. The sounds from last night, the drums… it could only mean one thing.

We weren't alone on this island.

Given the inhabited and native condition of this island, the idea of not being alone here gave me the willies. Who knew what else was living here? As if freefalling from the sky, crashing on a beach, having Nash stitch up my head with a needle, and having no food, water, or means of getting help wasn't scary enough, now we had to worry about some weird tribe of pigmies with machetes and weird beads in their dreads coming to make us some weird sacrifice in a pagan ritual. (What? I was dehydrated and hungry. You'd think strange things too.)

God. My life was so turning into one of those bad made-for-TV movies.

I was drained. After coming back to the plane last night, we sat huddled inside, listening for more strange sounds, both alert and ready for something bad to happen. I guess at some point, exhaustion won out and we both fell asleep.

Tossing off the blanket, I stretched out my wicked sore body and then went quickly into the cockpit. I knew it was probably a waste of time, but I had to try again.

I retrieved the broken radio from where Nash kicked it and sat down, tucking it into my lap. I pressed the buttons. I shook it around beside my ear, listening for—well, I don't know what I was listening for—and holding the microphone up to my mouth and calling for help.

Of course, nothing happened.

Well, actually, something did happen.

My panic got worse.

I tossed down the radio moved from the front of the plane, going back to where Nash was still sleeping. Nash was in one of the airline seats, his dark lashes fanned out over the dark circles that smudged beneath his eyes. He couldn't have been comfortable. He looked way too big for the chair he was slumped in.

He almost looked boyish sleeping like that. His hair was mussed, his body appeared boneless where it rested, and he had this air of innocence that wrapped around him, making my heart squeeze. However, the boyish comparisons ended the second my gaze settled on his lips. They were full and well-defined. The lower lip was curved and almost pouty, giving me an overwhelming urge to peruse them slowly with my own mouth. Just looking at them, thinking of how it felt to have those lips scorch my skin, made my body tingle.

I forced my stare away from him. This was no time to be having make-out thoughts about Nash. We were experiencing an emergency here. We needed a plan. We needed action. We needed coffee. I closed my eyes, wishing the tasty brew would magically appear in front of me. It didn't.

The grouchiness I'd been fighting came back full force. With a sigh, I moved quietly to the place I'd been marking the wall to help us keep track of the days. We were already on day three. Actually, more like day four or five, depending upon how long we both lay here after the crash. The tally read four because I was being optimistic that we hadn't lost more than one day.

Nash was still sleeping when I folded up my blanket and glanced longingly at the protein bars. My stomach rumbled loudly and I silently shushed it. I knew I couldn't eat one of those bars right now. It was probably better if we started splitting them in half instead of each eating a whole one.

It made me depressed, and it also made me worry. How long could someone of Nash's size go without food? I couldn't imagine how hungry he felt. It had to be far worse than the empty weakness I was feeling.

That gave me an idea. This was a semi-tropical climate. There had to be some kind of fruit growing on this island.

Yes, but fruit might not be the only thing on this island. I reminded myself. Going out there alone would be reckless. I might be blond, but I wasn't stupid. Okay,

I tried not to be stupid. Sometimes I wasn't very successful.

I should just wake him up. We could go out in search of food together.

I watched his chest rise and fall with his even breathing. I could wait a few more minutes. He looked so exhausted. I glanced out the back of the plane at the growing plants. Maybe there was some fruit close by, right outside the plane. Maybe I could find some and bring it back here to surprise him. I pictured the way his green eyes would light up when he saw the food.

That decided it. I was going. I would stay close, within yelling distance. If I didn't find anything, I would wake him and together we could search farther out.

I found my sandals and slipped them on, not wanting to be barefoot in the forest. I moved quietly toward the back of the plane, actually quite impressed with the stealth of my movements. Maybe when I got home, I should be a superhero.

Okay, maybe just a sidekick to a superhero.

I was about to leap out into the lush landscape when a strong arm snaked around my waist and pulled me back. "Where do you think you're going?" slurred a voice thick with sleep.

"To the bathroom," I lied.

"I'll come with you," he countered.

"I'm a big girl. I know how to use the bathroom."

"Maybe I need help," he said and shifted. Once again, I was met with the thing that lived inside his pants.

I gasped. "Does that thing ever go down?" I blurted out.

He threw back his head and laughed. He laughed so hard I felt his belly rumble against my back.

"I can't help it. It's my morning wood." He said it like he was proud.

"Your what?" I said, trying to turn around to look at him. He wouldn't let me go. If anything, he pressed it farther against me. Dammit if my body didn't start to respond. I felt the rush of liquid heat between my legs.

"My morning wood," he said again.

Should I know what that means? I guess when I failed to respond, he realized I had no clue what he was talking about. He spun me around, pinning me with that penetrating green gaze. "Have you ever spent the night with a man before?"

I acted like I was offended. "That's none of your business."

"That'd be a no."

I glared at him.

He released me. "It happens in sleep, sweetheart," he explained. "All men wake up with a hard on."

So it wasn't just me. Well, damn, there went my ego. "So *that* is natural?" I couldn't help but glance down at the massive lump in his shorts.

"In the morning, yes."

"But what about the other times?"

A slow smile spread over his scruffy face. "Those times were all you."

Oh. Oh my.

I wanted to pat my broken vagina on the back. If it had one, that is.

"Well, I'm going to go do my business now," I said, turning away.

"I'm coming with you."

"Why?" I demanded.

"Because I have to pee," he offered.

"Fine." My shoulders slumped and I hopped out of the plane.

"What's wrong with you?" he asked.

I heaved a sigh. "I wanted to go look for fruit for you before you woke up."

"You wanted to find me breakfast?"

I nodded. It sounded stupid when he said it.

He caught me around the waist again and tugged. I tumbled right against his chest. His very bare, shirtless chest. His lips swooped down, but his kiss wasn't like the impassioned one we shared yesterday. This one was softer, lighter. It caused a fluttering sensation inside me that made my heart stutter. I could literally feel it bouncing around beneath my ribcage.

Before he pulled away completely, he bestowed several brief kisses one right after the other, ending with one on the tip of my nose. "Thank you."

My hands rested over his chest against him warm skin. "I didn't do anything," I grumbled.

"I don't think going off on your own is a smart idea, especially after what we heard last night."

"I wasn't going off alone. I was just going to look right here, outside the plane." Why did saying that out loud make it seem like a dumb idea? I wondered if I dyed my hair brown would I get smarter...?

"Why don't we go look around for fruit together?" he suggested, making me forget my home makeover ideas.

I didn't answer because my stomach growled loudly, replying for me.

"I actually have to go to the bathroom. Don't go anywhere," he said, giving me a hard look.

Seconds later, he came back and disappeared into the plane to get some shoes and reappeared with all the empty water bottles, including the empty can of Coke. "Maybe we can find a freshwater source," he said, motioning to the bottles. "If not, we're going to have to start boiling some sea water."

I took a second to grab my messenger bag and slide it over my shoulders, slipping the bottles inside. I really hoped we found some food. I was so hungry I felt lightheaded.

"Stay close to me," Nash murmured as we traveled deeper into the florae. I gave him a sidelong glance, wondering if he was ever going to put a shirt back on. 'Course if he did, I would totally miss the view. The way his shorts hung low on his hips displayed his long, solid torso, and I think I might have started to drool a little.

I looked away. I was acting ridiculous. It was totally lack of food.

"What do you think that was last night?" I whispered, feeling like there were a million eyes staring at us as we moved.

"I'm not sure. It sounded a little like people and music."

I nodded. That's what I thought too. "But this place looks completely untouched."

"This side of the island. Maybe it's bigger than we realize and maybe on the other side there are people."

"Who would live way out here where there's nothing?" I wondered.

"Exactly," he said, his voice low like he hadn't wanted me to hear.

But I did. And it brought back that fear I felt last night.

A little while later, Nash stopped and tilted his head. "Hey, you hear that?"

I listened, not making out much over the loud chatter of the wildlife.

"It sounds like water."

I perked up and listened harder. It was very faint, but once he pointed it out, the sound was undeniable.

"This way."

He walked for what felt like hours (probably only minutes) and with each step, the sound of falling water drew closer and closer.

Nash pushed through very large plants with huge leaves and a few palm-looking trees and stopped. I ran right into his back because I wasn't paying any attention. I was too busy staring a beautiful pink flower close by.

He let out a whoop of joy and stepped to the side so I could see too. There just ahead lay a small lagoon-type pond and pouring into it was a short but wide waterfall.

Both of us rushed forward toward the water, but something caught my eye and I turned. Oval-shaped green fruit grew from a plant very close by. I changed course and rushed over, plucking one of the fruits and palming it. It was about the size of my hand and boasted a fresh green skin.

It was an avocado.

I'd never seen any of these plants in person before. This was something we could live on. It was full of healthy fats and fiber, something that would definitely help keep Nash from starving.

"Ava?" Nash called.

I looked over my shoulder with a smile, only to realize I'd gotten farther away from him than I thought. I hadn't even paid attention I was so intent on getting to the food.

"Ava," he called again, more urgency to his voice. He wasn't in sight anymore, but I heard the water splash.

"Over here," I shouted, not wanting him to worry.

"Where?"

"I found food!" I exclaimed, turning to rush back the way I came. My foot caught on a huge root growing up out of the earth and I tripped, the fruit in my arms tumbling to the ground, and I cried out as I fell.

Someone caught the back of my shirt, literally grasping the fabric and halting my plunge forward. Before I could make sense of what was happening, an arm looped around my middle and the hand released my shirt. As I was pulled upright, I turned, wondering how in the world Nash found me so fast.

It wasn't Nash.

It was another man.

The arm at my waist tightened when I looked into his dark eyes.

I screamed.

8

I heard my name being yelled and the thrashing of foliage behind me, but I didn't look. I was transfixed by this new pair of dark-brown eyes.

"Whoa," he said, his voice sounding so foreign to my ears. After days of hearing no one speak but Nash, this was a little startling.

"Are you okay?" he asked. His sweeping gaze reminded me of the coffee I so desperately missed. I opened my mouth to answer, but I never got the chance. I was ripped away from the rich stare. Nash pushed me behind him and then drew his fist back like he was going to plant it in this guy's face.

"Wait!" I said, grabbing him just below the elbow to restrain him. His muscles strained beneath my palm and I thought he might follow through with the hit, but he held back. "He didn't hurt me. I tripped and he was helping me up."

My words sank in as Nash dropped his hand and flexed his fist at his side. Then he nodded curtly.

The man hadn't said anything at all. He just watched us both like he was utterly fascinated. Like he hadn't seen a person in a very long time.

Maybe he hadn't.

"Who are you?" I asked, curious, stepping out around Nash, who brought out his arm to keep me from getting any closer.

"My name's Duke," the man replied, gazing at me intently. He had a very even, unwavering stare when he looked at me. It was like I was the only thing in this world.

He was also very tan, like Nash, but his hair was straight and a lighter shade of brown, like a deep caramel color. It was long, brushing the back of his shirt, the ends flipping up and the rest tucked behind his ears. He had a straight, prominent nose and full lips. But the most captivating feature on his face was his eyes, deep and mysterious. I had a feeling I could stare into those eyes for hours and still not be any closer to figuring out what went on behind them.

He was tall, but not nearly as tall as Nash. He was probably a few inches taller than me. He wasn't a huge guy, but he wasn't real small either. He was thin and it made me wonder if it was because he was being held captive by this place like us—except he'd been here longer.

He definitely appeared more at ease here, and his clothes showed signs of wear. He was wearing a white T-shirt that was no longer quite white. It hung loose over a pair of jeans that were frayed around the ankles, and his feet were bare. His right cheek boasted a smear of dirt and I had the urge to brush it away.

And then I noticed the scar.

I was surprised I hadn't noticed it sooner, being just above his left eye, cutting through the center of his eyebrow. But I supposed the fact I hadn't noticed was just proof as to how striking and interesting the rest of him was.

"Are you alone here, Duke?" Nash asked, a hint of suspicion in his tone.

Duke nodded, not looking away from me. "I was out fishing and got lost at sea. Ended up here. If anyone came looking for me, they never found me."

Dread settled at the bottom of my stomach, weighing me down. "How long have you been here?" I asked, hollow.

"I've lost track of time. Months."

Oh my God. *Months?* He'd been stranded here all alone for months?

Nash's hand found mine and he threaded our fingers together and gave mine a little squeeze as if to say, *That's not going to be us.*

But how could he know? If this island managed to keep one person here, then why not two more?

Duke finally turned his stare to Nash. "You're new here."

Nash nodded. "Our plane went down." He pointed in the direction of the beach. "Over on that side of the island. We've been here about four days."

"Will people be looking for you?" Duke asked.

"Yes," Nash answered. There wasn't a hint of doubt in his voice.

Duke bent down and picked up one of the avocados that I dropped and extended it to me. "You dropped this."

"Thank you." I took it and put it on display for Nash. "Look, avocado."

He pulled his hand out of mine and placed it on my lower back possessively. "Good job, *Bella*." The last word he drawled in Spanish.

I liked it, but I wondered if he only called me that to send a message to Duke. Why was he behaving that way?

"You're hungry?" Duke said, looking at me.

"Yeah, we've been looking for food."

"I know where coconuts and mangos grow."

A little moan of desire escaped my lips. "Will you show us?"

"Of course. The fruit is farther that way on the island." He pointed off in the direction away from the plane.

"Let's gather as many of these as we can," I suggested. "And take them back to the plane. Then we can go gather some fruit."

Nash seemed a little hesitant at first, but then he relented. The lure of fresh fruit was too strong to deny. "Is the water here drinkable?" Nash asked, gesturing back toward the little lagoon and waterfall.

"Yes," Duke said, nodding his head. A lock of hair slipped free of his ear and brushed against his stubbled cheek.

The light scruff coating his jaw caught my attention. "I'm surprised you don't have a full beard from being here so long," I said.

"Eh, I've always been lousy at growing a beard." He grinned and scratched at his chin.

I found myself smiling back at him.

"We can fill up our bottles too," Nash said, his voice sounding slightly annoyed.

Stirred back to the task at hand, I started gathering the fruit, piling my bag full. There was one piece that looked particularly enticing and it was just out of reach. I stood on my tiptoes, extending my arm, but I just couldn't seem to stretch far enough.

"Here," Duke said, coming up behind me. His voice was deep and it brushed against the back of my head. He stepped close, his chest brushing my back, and reached up, plucking the food from the tree. As he pulled down his arm, he brushed against the bare skin of my arm. Little tingles of awareness shot along my skin.

I stepped back a little, looking between him and his offering. "Don't you want to keep any for yourself?"

He shook his head slowly. "I already have some saved up. You take it."

"Thank you." I tucked it beneath my arm. "Where do you... umm... live? Did you build a shelter?"

"I did, but a storm came through last month and it was lost. I pretty much stay wherever now."

I couldn't imagine being here through a tropical storm. That had to have been so scary. And to be alone. At least Nash and I had each other. I glanced at him and noted that he was no longer gathering fruit. He was watching Duke and me.

"We could help you build a new one," I offered. "Since you're showing us where to find the mangos and coconuts."

"You would do that?" Duke asked, his eyes sweeping over me.

"Of course."

"Ava," Nash called. "Come on. We need to get some water."

The three of us made our way back to the lagoon, where I pulled out the empty water bottles and cans. The water was cool against my fingers and I plunged them down deep, enjoying the icy freshness of water without salt. My mouth almost ached for a taste, as we'd been rationing our water and soda intake since we arrived.

I cupped my hands and filled my palms with the liquid and brought them up near my face.

"Wait," Nash spoke softly, crouching down beside me. His hand stilled my own. Then he pulled away, reached into the water and got his own drink, sipping it into his mouth and swirling it around his tongue.

I had a sudden desire to be that water.

Then he swallowed. He took another drink. I started to lift my hands again, almost desperate for a drink, and he stopped me again.

I made a sound of frustration. "I'm thirsty."

"I know," he said softly, bringing up his dampened thumb and sweeping it across my lip. Automatically, my tongue came out, licking off the moisture and pulling the pad of his thumb into my mouth.

"I told you it's safe to drink," muttered a voice from the other side of me. Startled, I pulled away, releasing Nash's thumb.

"I wanted to make sure," Nash said, his voice holding a hint of annoyance.

"You were testing the water out on yourself!" I exclaimed, pinning him with an gaping stare.

"I doubt it would do much good," he said. "If it's going to make me sick, it won't be for a while."

"I'm so thirsty," I whined, not caring I sounded like a child.

Duke made a sound, drawing my attention. He cupped his hand in the water and took a great gulp. "See?" he said. "I've been drinking this since I got here. It's never made me sick."

Then he reached out and guided my hands back into the water. It lapped over our skin, swirling around us. I looked up at him. His face was so close to mine. He smiled.

Nash cleared his throat.

I pulled up my hands, Duke keeping his palm cupped beneath mine, and I drank. The fresh, icy water slid down my parched throat and I sighed. It was heavenly.

I drank more, feeling like I couldn't get enough. Then I splashed it over my face and neck, feeling more refreshed than I had when I cleaned off in the ocean the day before.

Once the bottles were filled, the three of us set off toward the plane, Nash and I eating an avocado in record time. Nash was fairly quiet, only interrupting Duke's and my chattering to ask questions about the island.

Turns out Duke had no idea where we were either. He wasn't sure how far the closest civilized location could be.

I opened my mouth to ask him if he heard the same sounds we had the night before, or if he knew if we were the only ones here, but Nash caught my eye and gave me slight shake of his head. For some reason he didn't want me to say anything. So I didn't.

Duke was fascinated with the plane and once he realized Nash was a pilot, he peppered him with a million questions. Nash didn't seem to mind. I could tell how passionate about flying he was. How much he loved it. I puttered around, placing the fruit inside with the water and glancing at the remaining protein bars longingly.

When that was done, I came outside where Nash and Duke stood talking quietly.

Nash looked up, noticing me first, palming one of the bottles of water. "Ready?"

I nodded, my stomach grumbling with the promise of fresh fruit.

"So, Duke," I began as we followed him to the food, "where are you from?"

"I've lived in Puerto Rico and many of the islands in the area."

"What did you do for a living before...?" My voice trailed away.

"Before I was lost at sea?" he finished, sounding less upset about it than I might have. I wondered if we never were found if I would come to accept it. My gut said no. I didn't want this to be all there was. I didn't want my family to think I had died a horrible death.

"Yeah," I said, realizing it might be easier not to ask him questions.

"I gave guided boat tours. Mostly to tourists."

"You must be really familiar with the area, then," Nash observed.

He glanced over his shoulder. "That's the thing. The ocean covers all its tracks. It drowns all its landmarks. The sea is ever changing, always moving. It's a lot harder than one might think to learn the 'lay of the land' here because there isn't much land." But then he looked at me and winked. "But I've been on this island long enough to know where the good eats are."

I smiled.

We walked forever it seemed. Although, maybe it wasn't as long as it felt because I was impatient. I wanted to eat. Finally, Duke pointed just ahead to a bunch of greenery (that looked a lot like everything else we'd already passed) and announced the sustenance was up ahead.

The trees around use were heavy with ripe mangos. The yellowish-green-colored skin was a beacon to my belly. The only time I'd ever eaten a mango was after I'd sliced it up and peeled off the skin. Those luxuries didn't apply here. I was starving and all I cared about was getting something in my very empty belly.

I plucked one off a tree and rubbed it on my shirt, about to bite in, but I stopped. I turned, seeking out Nash and spotting him just yards away. As I moved closer, he must have sensed my presence because he turned toward me.

I held out the fruit, offering it to him. His lips pulled up in a half smile as he leaned forward and took a bite out of the juicy flesh, still leaving it in my hand. Nectar slid down his lips, but he caught it with his tongue, dragging the sweetness back into his mouth. I watched, transfixed, forgetting I was hungry for food as a different desire swept over me.

His body stiffened as he chewed and a choking sound ripped from his throat. He wrapped his hands around his neck as his eyes bulged.

"Nash?"

He made a gurgling sound.

I looked at the mango in my hand… wondering if maybe it wasn't a mango at all.

Maybe it was poisoned.

9

Alarm slammed into me and I threw down the fruit and reached out for him. "Nash!" I cried, so afraid he was going to die and there would be nothing I could do to save him.

Seeing my genuine fear, he dropped his hands and caught me by the shoulders. "I'm fine."

"Are you poisoned?" I demanded, adrenaline still pumping through my limbs.

"I was only kidding."

"Here, drink some water! Rinse out your mouth," I said, yanking the water from his pocket and thrusting it at him.

"Ava!" he said sternly, taking hold of my wrists. "I'm fine. It was a joke."

His words finally penetrated my anxiety and I stared at him, astonished. Then anger took hold and I smacked at his chest. "That was mean!" I squealed. "My God, you scared me half to death."

His brows drew together. "I'm sorry. I really didn't mean to scare you. I was teasing."

Duke pushed his way between us, inserting his body in front of mine, and gave Nash a shove. "What the hell is wrong with you?" he growled. "Did you see how scared she was?"

I felt tears prick the back of my eyes and I pushed them away. Any other time I would have laughed. It would have been funny. But not here. Not now.

"You're a douche," Duke said, crossing his arms across his chest.

I stepped out around him and looked at Nash, whose jaw was working overtime, his back teeth grinding furiously. He caught me looking and pulled me against him roughly, wrapping me in his arms. "I'm sorry," he murmured, rubbing my back. "I wasn't thinking."

I made a sound against his chest. What would I do here without him? What would I do if he was seriously hurt or worse? I felt my body shake and I tried to control it. I tried not to worry.

Nash reached between us, titling up my chin with his hands. "I'm not going anywhere," he promised softly. "I'm an ass. Forgive me." Then he pressed an ultra-light, ultra-brief kiss to my lips.

Just that brief contact made me feel better.

"It's okay. I didn't mean to freak out."

Behind me, Duke snorted. Nash's eyes flicked over my shoulder but then back to me as he yanked another mango free and wiped it on his shoulder, pressing it against my lips. "Eat."

I forgot all about his joke and tore into the succulent fruit. I ate it in what seemed like seconds flat. Then he handed me another. "You too," I told him, watching as he grabbed a couple and started chowing down.

I wandered through the fruit trees, eating and filling up my messenger bag until it was swollen and packed with the fruit. I caught sight of Duke at the edge of my vision and he motioned for me to join him.

When I stopped at his side, he pointed to a few palm trees reaching up into the sunlight. "There's your coconuts," he said.

I made a sound of disappointment. "They're so high up."

"I'll get you one."

"You can get those?" I asked, doubt lacing my tone.

"What will you give me if I do?" he asked, a hint of playfulness catching my attention. I smiled.

"I won't turn into a cannibal and eat you," I promised with mock seriousness.

He threw back his head and laughed.

"So are you any good at climbing palm trees?" I crossed my arms over my chest and studied him.

Duke leaned close and whispered. "I've got lots of hidden talents."

The shot of heat in my belly shocked me. I felt my eyes widen.

He chuckled and handed me a few mangos he was holding. Then he shimmied up the trunk of the palm tree.

I stood there and watched in awe. He was like a living monkey. I could tell he was very adept at this and he moved quickly, so quickly that I was amazed by his agility.

"Look out below!" he called when he reached the top. I shrieked and ran for cover as coconuts rained from the tree.

Within minutes, he was back down on the ground and I rushed to gather everything that rolled beneath the foliage. I made a little pile beneath the tree and then went after the last one that was deep beneath a broad leaf.

When I pulled back, he was right there, practically on top of me. I jerked back. "Geesh. You're quick."

"Practice," he said, shrugging his shoulders.

"Thank you for this."

"And now for the payment," he murmured, his gaze dropping to my lips.

The bottom of my stomach fell out.

Did he want me to kiss him?

"Uhhh," I said, unsure what to do. My eyes automatically looked for Nash.

"Right here," Duke said, tapping a finger to his cheek.

I grinned in relief. Holding the coconut between us, I leaned up and pressed a kiss to his cheek. I pulled back, but not all the way, our eyes connecting. Something shifted between us. I could feel his desire, his want for me.

It was heady and intoxicating.

"Ava," Nash called, appearing out of nowhere.

I jerked and stepped back, rushing to show him the coconuts. I couldn't help but notice the narrowed-eyed stare he gave Duke when he thought I wasn't looking.

"Look!" I exclaimed, motioning to the pile of fuzzy coconuts.

"Now we just have to crack them open," Nash said ruefully.

"I can help with that," Duke cut in.

I spun. "You can?"

He nodded. "Come on." We each gathered up a couple coconuts and then set off on foot again, following behind Duke. I could feel Nash's curious stare on me from time to time, but I didn't acknowledge it. I wasn't sure I wanted to know what he was trying to figure out.

We came to a little area that seemed to have more dense foliage than the other places around us. Duke ducked inside a little area of palm fronds that had grown together closely, making a sort of shelter. Seconds later, he appeared carrying a machete.

"Here, you can use this." He extended it to me.

"Really?"

He nodded. I took the handle, surprised at the weight. "Thank you."

"Where did you get that?" Nash asked.

"Found it."

"But if we take this, what will you use?"

He shrugged. "I can use that one. It will give me an excuse to come visit you."

I smiled.

"We should probably start back." Nash cut in quickly.

"I'll show you the way," Duke offered and started out ahead of us, leading us back the way we came. On the way through the mango trees, I grabbed a couple more and feasted.

By the time we arrived back at the plane, the sky was darkening and the cicadas were starting their evening song.

"Where did the day go?" I asked, placing all the food beside the plane.

"You're on island time now." Duke reminded me with a grin.

I picked up a coconut, studying it and wondering how hard it was going to be to break into.

"Here," Duke said, taking it from me and retrieving the machete from where Nash had leaned it before going off to the men's room (aka: over behind a tree).

I wasn't surprised when he used the tool expertly. I was beginning to realize that Duke was a wealth of skill and information. He could very well help us survive out here.

A minute later, he handed me the coconut. The top had a few layers peeled away and a gash in the tip. "Drink the liquid first. Then I'll split it open and you can eat the flesh inside."

"Would you like one too?" I gestured toward the mini mountain.

He shook his head. "You keep them. I ate a couple earlier."

The slightly sweet, creamy liquid of the coconut hit my tongue in a burst of flavor. I groaned in appreciation and tilted it back farther, taking more into my mouth.

Duke chuckled. "That's good, huh?"

"You have no idea," I murmured and then went back for more.

He watched me like I was an entertaining show on TV, and I found that his gaze didn't make me uncomfortable. I didn't feel self-conscious around him like I sometimes did with people I just met. I already felt like he and I were bonded. And maybe we already were. After all, we all had one very big thing in common. We were survivors.

When all the liquid was drained away, he took the coconut from me and split it in half, revealing layers of pure-white fruit.

Nash came to my side and I offered him a bite of the fruit I was already gobbling up. He scooped a little onto his fingers, but he didn't eat it. Instead, he offered it to me.

I opened my mouth and he placed his fingers inside as my lips clamped down. Slowly, he slid them out. Then he looked at Duke pointedly.

Was that some kind of message?

Was he... was he jealous?

I sighed and walked away. I wasn't interested in being the prize in any kind of macho game. Part of me was tempted to yell back that whoever "won" me would end up with a faulty prize, but I thought better of it and kept my mouth shut.

I carried my snack down to the beach where I kicked off my shoes and sat down in the sand. One nice thing about being stranded on an island: the sunsets were awesome.

A few moments later, Duke and Nash joined me, one sitting on each side of me. The three of us sat there quietly, watching the sun turn the waves a burnished gold.

When darkness became heavier, Duke looked at the little place we had a bonfire the night before. "Want me to help you get a fire started?"

Nash paused. "I'm not sure it's safe."

Duke considered his words for a moment. "It's safe. Just don't make it too big."

I glanced at him, thinking surely he must know what we were talking about.

"Are you sure?" Nash said.

Duke glanced at me, then back at Nash. "Yeah. I'm sure. It gets chilly here when the sun goes down."

The two guys worked side by side and soon had a small fire crackling. Nash called to me and I got up, wandering closer to the flickering flames, drawn to their warmth and comfort.

"Well, I should be going," Duke began, turning to me. "You going to be okay?"

I nodded. "You don't want to stay?"

I felt Nash's stare, but I refused to acknowledge him. If Duke wanted to stay here, then he was welcome. I wasn't sure what Nash's problem was, but he could get over it. We needed to stick together. Maybe the three of us could figure out a way off this island and back home.

Duke gave me a half smile that melted my heart a little. There was a flash of longing in his eyes and I thought he might agree. But then he shook his head.

I frowned, automatically reaching out and taking his hand. "You're welcome to stay here with us. The plane is good shelter."

"Thank you," he said, giving my fingers a light squeeze. "But I'm used to where I sleep. I'll think about it though, okay?"

I nodded. He released my hand and stepped back, glanced at Nash, and nodded a good-bye.

"Wait," I called when he would have walked away.

He glanced over his shoulder, his dark molten eyes sweeping my face. "I'll be back tomorrow."

I nodded and he departed. Just as the darkness was about to conceal him completely, he turned back. "Whatever you do, don't go on the other side of the island."

Chills raced up my back and they weren't the good kind.

Then he stepped through the cover of night and completely disappeared. I let out a shaky breath and looked at Nash. He was staring after him with an unreadable expression on his face.

"All right," I began. "What gives?"

His eyebrows rose halfway up his forehead and disappeared beneath the dark curls. "What do you mean?"

I rolled my eyes. "Don't give me that innocent act," I intoned. "You know exactly what I mean. Duke was nothing but nice to us. He helped us find food and he gave us that machete."

"I don't like him," he said simply, sitting down in one of the chairs by the fire.

"Why not?"

"Besides the fact that he just alluded to the fact he knows there's something bad on the other side of the island and didn't tell us?" he said, making chills race up my spine once more.

"Yeah," I said dryly. "Besides that." Because that just happened. Nash had been acting like Duke was trying to kill us since we first laid eyes on him.

"He wants you."

I made a startled sound. "What?"

He stared at me intently. "You can't honestly tell me you didn't see the way he looked at you."

"He's just lonely," I said. "He's been here all alone."

He made a rude sound.

I tossed my arm out to smack him. He caught it, folding it across his chest and holding it there. "He wants you, Ava," he rumbled. "But he can't have you."

"He can't?" I asked, my voice shaky.

He shook his head slowly. "No. He can't. You're already taken."

10

My tongue jetted out, wetting my lips. "You think I'm taken?" Never mind the fact my words sounded breathless and I could barely hear myself speak over the pounding of my own heart.

"I *know* you are. You just haven't realized it yet."

"You're not going to want me when we get home and there are a lot of other options," I said, surprising myself with the comeback. Usually, I didn't just blurt out those things. Even so, it was true. Maybe if I had been more assertive with my thoughts in the past, I wouldn't have gotten so hurt. The only reason I looked so good right now was because I was the only girl within a hundred-mile radius.

He turned his head away from the fire and pinned me with his jade stare. "You said certain parts of you are broken."

I didn't say anything. I just held his gaze.

"What parts are you talking about, Ava?"

I reached up and played with the ends of the thick braid falling over my shoulder, twisting the strands around my finger. I wasn't really sure I wanted to have this conversation. It wasn't something I cared to talk about—to even think about. Of course maybe if I told him, he would decide he didn't want me after all and it would save me from the pain later.

Because Nash had the power to hurt me.

He was the kind of guy that would steal away my heart when I wasn't looking. He was the kind of guy who would love me so well that when he left, no one would ever be able to take his place and so I would walk around the rest of my life with a huge chunk of myself missing because it would always belong to him.

I turned in the crappy aircraft seat that was now a makeshift beach chair. I drew my knees into my chest and rested the side of my head against the seat, looking at him through the orange glow of the bonfire.

"I dated a guy once," I began, speaking only loud enough so he could hear. He didn't look at me but stared straight ahead out over the waves as the breeze ruffled through those dark, touchable curls. "He was sweet, funny, the kind of guy that my mother approved of. Everyone liked him. I liked him. After a couple months of dating, he wanted to take our relationship to the next step. I said no. So we kept dating. He sent me flowers, took me on dates… Sometimes his touches would linger a little too long or his hands would be a little too rough. He told me I was just being a prude, that every other girl liked it. Every other part of our relationship was great. I just couldn't seem to get into…" My voice faded away. I wasn't sure how to explain it.

"He didn't turn you on," Nash said, putting it simply. It seemed much simpler when he said it than how it felt when I was living through it.

"I guess."

"What happened?" he said, still not looking at me. I couldn't help but notice the way the muscles in his shoulders bunched, the way the side of his jaw ticked every so often.

He probably already figured out which parts of me didn't work.

"Long story short, I gave in. I slept with him. It was awful. He broke up with me the next day and told everyone I was cold."

He turned his head and looked at me.

His expression was unreadable.

"I haven't dated anyone since."

"How does that make you broken?"

I paused. "Clearly there are parts of me that don't work the way... the way men want them to. Not to mention the skewed view I now have about dating."

He stood. He was going to walk away. This conversation was over.

But he touched me.

He started at my shoulder and trailed his finger down my arm and then cupped my elbow, gently tugging me out of the chair and onto my feet.

We stood at the edge of the crackling bonfire, facing each other. Everything in our little circle was bathed in a yellow and orange glow, the shadows reaching into the complete darkness beyond—like nothing else existed at all.

Slowly he tugged the tie around my braid, tucking the scrap of fabric in the pocket of his shorts. Using just one hand, he unbound the weave, then pulled his fingers through the waves, spreading it out around me so it cascaded over my shoulders and covered up my chest.

"Did you feel that?" he murmured, releasing my hair and trailing his hands down my arms until he came to the hem of my T-shirt.

Oh, I felt it.

I felt it deep into my bones. All he had to do was look at me and I felt *everything* times ten.

His eyes looked deep into mine as he lifted my shirt, the cooling night air brushing over my waist. "Up," was his soft command.

I lifted my arms and he slid the cotton over my head, making sure it didn't come into contact with my stitches. He tossed it away, out of the golden bubble we were in, the blackness swallowing it as if it ceased to exist.

He stepped forward, eliminating the distance between us. The only thing separating our chests from contact was the fabric of my bikini top. He took my hand and lifted it, placing it right over his heart, flattening my palm and holding it there.

He leaned closer so his lips brushed against the hair covering my ear.

"Can you feel my heart pounding?"

I swallowed and nodded. It was pounding... so hard that its rhythm matched mine.

Still pressing my hand against the smoothness of his skin, he dragged our hands lower, down his pec, across his defined abs, and then hooked them around his waist. When he pulled his hand away, mine stayed, flexing over his flesh, my fingers refusing to let go.

He flirted with the waistband of my shorts, tugging at it, then smoothing it back into place. Lightly he dragged his fingers up, climbing like a spider over my ribs until his hands rested just below my breasts.

Instead of traveling upward, he went around, fingers fiddling with the strings that held my top in place.

His forehead leaned against mine. I could hear his breathing, slightly uneven, as the heat from the fire enveloped us. "I'm going to kiss you now," he whispered. "And I'm going to put my hands all over your body. You're going to feel every single thing I do to you and then you're going to beg me not to stop."

He swallowed my reply, kissing me so profoundly it was as if he completely understood the inner workings of my body. The kiss wasn't deep, but it reached so far inside me that I no longer knew where I ended and he began. He cupped my face, angling it up so he could sweep his tongue along mine until they tangled together so intimately I groaned.

As we kissed, he pulled the string behind my back, untying my top. When it didn't fall away, his hands delved into my hair and found the other bow, tugging, and the top fell between us, landing in the sand.

My breasts brushed against his chest and I gasped at the skin-on-skin contact. My nipples hardened instantly and became more sensitive than I ever thought possible. But their sensitivity didn't make me pull away; it made me arch into him farther.

He growled low in his throat. The sound vibrated from his mouth and into mine, echoing deep inside me. His hands cupped my butt, kneading its softness and tilting my hips forward so I could feel his rock-hard erection pressing against me urgently.

I purred. Like a contented cat.

I gripped his waist, trying to pull him closer. He just wasn't close enough.

He ripped his mouth free of mine and lifted me; my legs wound around his waist. Instead of letting me fall against him, he held me out and suckled my breast into his mouth. I jerked against him. The sensation of his hot, wet mouth upon me sent a rush of fiery tingles throughout my body. It was like his mouth was in one place, but I felt him *everywhere*.

The ocean breeze carried away my moan as my head fell back and the ends of my hair brushed against my waist. When he lifted his head, I grabbed at him, delving my fingers deep into his mane of hair, finally touching the curls that had called to me since I laid eyes on them. They were softer than I imagined and they curled around my fingers, claiming them, as if everything I had wasn't already his.

His mouth moved to my other breast and he licked beneath it, a long drawn out drag of his tongue on the underside. His mouth traveled upward, nipping lightly at the creamy flesh before closing over my nipple and causing jolts of pleasure so intense that it felt like I was being electrocuted.

No one had ever put his mouth on me before like this.

He languished attention on my chest until I was making small mewling noises and both our bodies were shaking. Totally weak and turned on, I collapsed against his chest, managing to keep one hand tangled in his hair.

"I'm not done with you yet," he murmured and sank to his knees right there beside the fire. Gently, he laid me on my back, my blond locks fanning out around my head and across the sand.

"You still with me?" he murmured, his body hovering over mine.

I opened my eyes and gazed up at him. He was utterly gorgeous. He was everything I ever wanted and never thought I would have. Not because I wasn't good enough for someone like him, but because I didn't think feelings like this actually existed.

"Yes," I said, reaching up and running my hands across his chest. "I'm with you."

His mouth claimed mine once more, searing my soul and trailing down into the hollow of my neck, leaving a scorching path behind him.

My skin would never be the same after this.

It would forever echo with the memory of how he made me hum. Desire curled through me, rising up like steam on a humid rainy day and filling me up until I craved something more, but I had no idea what more there could possibly be.

He started to whisper words I didn't understand, words that sounded like a song rolling off his tongue, carrying across my skin, and sinking in… right into my heart. In between all his whispered words of romance, he pressed kisses like he was following a map to a destination that only he knew.

When he reached the inside of my thigh, I tensed, not sure what he planned on doing. He rocked back on his knees, kneeling over me like a god conquering a new possession.

And dear Lord, I wanted to be possessed by him.

He watched me closely as he slid the black linen shorts down my legs, yanking them free of my body. He skimmed his hands up my thighs. "You are unbelievably soft," he whispered.

I shivered.

"Tell me what you feel," he said, sneaking his hands beneath the ties at the sides of my hips.

I moaned. He expected me to speak?

"Ava, tell me," he commanded, pulling away his touch completely.

"I feel like my skin is on fire and you're the only thing that can cool me down."

He smiled. His gaze was heavy as he came over me, supporting his weight on his hands on either side of my body. "Did he touch you like this, *bella?*" he asked, his eyes were heavy with desire. "Did you want him so badly you could barely think?"

"Who?" I asked, not wanting to talk. Talking was clearly overrated.

He chuckled. "Good answer."

He lowered until our bodies brushed together and then he moved down, dragging his skin across mine, and I arched up, the touch driving me insane. He grasped the strings at my hips, and tugged, but he didn't pull the bottoms away.

"Can I see you, Ava? Can I see all of you?"

"Please," I whispered, rolling my hips.

The night air brushed over my newly bared skin and once again he whispered something in Spanish. It sounded like a prayer.

His fingers played with the nest of short curls between my legs, tugging and caressing. My eyes opened wide, shock rippling through me. *He was going to touch me there?*

Instead of feeling insecure and embarrassed, I was curious. I wanted to know the kinds of pleasure he could elicit with a single touch.

I didn't have to wait long. He drew two fingers down the center of me, his fingertips gliding through the silky wetness that my body was pumping out to excess.

He groaned. "You're soaked."

Before I could say anything or wonder if that was good or bad, those two naughty fingers slipped *inside* me. My back arched up off the sand and I grabbed for something to anchor me to the ground because surely I was going to float away.

In and out, in and out, his fingers worked me, my muscles contracting around them, begging for more. I was panting. The sensations rippling through my body were unmatched. It was the single most pleasurable feeling I had ever known.

And then he kissed me. Down there.

As his fingers worked, stretching out my entrance, his tongue began to lick at my folds, delving around, looking for something. Something I really wanted him to find.

My hips started to move, pumping up against him, moving with his rhythm. And then his mouth closed over the hardened bud deep at my center. He tugged and gently sucked at it. I cried out.

His fingers slid out of me, skimming up my center and leaving behind a trail of moisture. I was trembling, my skin was vibrating, and I couldn't lie still. I had to move. I had to get there.

"What do you want, *bella*?" he drawled from between my thighs.

I couldn't tell him because I didn't know. I was floating around in unchartered territory and I was solely dependent on him to show me the way. I whimpered.

He flattened his palms, one on each thigh, and pushed my legs wide, completely opening me up to him. And then he came forward, delving his tongue into my opening, his mouth connecting with my most secret place.

I bucked up. The feeling was so intense. He clamped down on my hips, pinning them into the sand, refusing to let me move. And then he licked up, one long, firm stroke, and my entire world shattered.

He held me down as I cried out, blinding white light exploding behind my eyes, completely decimating thought and knowledge of everything and anything. I wanted to squirm around so badly, but he wouldn't let me. I had to lie there beneath him, next to the fire and the sand at my back, and do nothing but let the orgasm roll over my body relentlessly.

When at last my body quieted and the sound of the crashing waves filled my ears, I lay back, completely boneless and breathing heavily.

Nash came over me once more, his curls falling over his forehead. "You, *mi bella,* are not broken. You are fucking perfect. So hot I almost came in my shorts."

"I want to see you."

One eyebrow lifted. "Do you now?"

I nodded.

I'd never felt so relaxed in my entire life. He rocked back between my legs and reached for the button on his shorts. I pushed up onto my elbows to watch.

He gazed at me, tenderness filling his eyes. "We can stop right here. We don't have to go any further. Your pleasure is my pleasure. It's more than enough for me."

I believed him. He would stop and he wouldn't get angry and he wouldn't tell me I was cold. "I don't want to stop."

I sat up the rest of the way and reached for his button, fully intending on experiencing everything I possibly could with him.

In that moment, a sound cut through the darkness.

It was the kind of sound that completely obliterated the passion surrounding us, the kind of sound that had Nash diving on top of me to shield my body from any harm.

We lay there silently until all went still and I was wondering if maybe we had imagined it. But then it pierced the night again.

We weren't hearing things.

We were hearing gunshots.

11

Nothing like the fear of being shot in your slumber to ruin a perfectly good night. After we heard those two shots penetrate the night, we gathered our clothes (okay, so they were my clothes) and hurried back to the plane.

Nash shielded me the entire way.

Once inside, I slipped on an oversized T-shirt I had in my suitcase and a pair of panties. Nash stood in the back of the plane, staring out into the darkness for a long time. After a long while of hearing nothing, we laid out all the blankets we could find on the floor against the wall and then lay down with a pillow and used the remaining blanket to cover us.

It was the first night I slept with him.

Well, in his arms.

It was the first time I lay all night with a warm body pressed against mine and an arm draped over my waist. Whenever I moved, he moved. Whenever I shifted, his body would follow. It's like we were two giant human magnets that couldn't be separated.

Yes, we were stranded and alone. We had very little food, very little water. We had no TV, no cell phone, and our choices for sleeping were limited to uncomfortable chairs or the floor of a plane. And yet...

I'd never been more comfortable.

It was a little unsettling to realize that just the mere presence of one person could make up for every comfort and convenience you thought you could never live without.

* * *

The sun was up when I stretched against him, my first thought being that we made it through another night without being attacked by weirdoes with machetes. The weight of being stranded on this island threatened to crush me, and I had to take a deep breath. How many more days would we be here? We needed a plan, some kind of hope that we wouldn't end up trapped here forever.

Or worse.

As I worried, a hand stroked over my hip. My shirt had ridden up during the night and Nash caressed my bare skin. "Good morning," he murmured, his voice thick with sleep.

"Hi." I tried not to notice his morning "wood," as he put it, but it was kind of hard to miss. I had to admit, it *was* a good distraction from my mental state of chaos.

"Did you get any sleep last night?"

I nodded. I wasn't about to admit how freaked out I really was. It wouldn't make anything better. And besides that, I might not have gotten a ton of sleep, but lying here, crushed up against him, was better than sleep. My brain might be in desperate need of a chill pill, but my body was more relaxed that it had ever been—even after we heard the somber firing of a gun.

Just the mere memory of what Nash and I did last night had heat wrapping around my insides, a slow burn igniting somewhere within me.

He didn't seem to notice the way he affected me. His hand slid up to rest at the dip in my waist as his thumb slid back and forth over my skin. I shivered. He pressed a kissed to my forehead.

"Are you hungry?"

I nodded. I was *so* hungry.

He moved away, leaving me lying there all alone, and my eyes popped open. He came back seconds later and sat down, Indian style, in front of me. I rolled onto my back and looked up as he dangled the Luna bar in the air.

He had one in each hand.

I gasped. "We're going to eat them?"

He gave a little shrug. "We have all the fruit and avocado now. I think it would be okay if we indulged this one time and each ate one."

I groaned. An entire bar all to myself? Heaven.

I reached for it and he snatched it away.

"Hey!" I demanded.

"You didn't tell me good morning yet."

"Yes, I did."

"Hi, does not count."

I pursed my lips while watching him. He had this little twinkle in his eye, and scorching heat swept me anew. I sat up, the blanket falling around my lap, and scooted so our knees bumped. Then I leaned forward and kissed the underside of his jaw.

He hadn't been able to shave since we crashed and the short beard he was sporting tickled my lips. I kissed him again, going down his neck.

"Wrong direction," he whispered, his voice husky.

My, he was demanding in the morning.

I changed course, kissing back up his neck, across his jaw, and then rubbing my cheek against his, enjoying the scruffy feel on my face. Then I turned my head and grazed his lips with mine. Before I pulled back, my hand went into his lap and grabbed at the bar he was holding.

He dropped the bar, but his newly free hand came up to wrap around the back of my head and hold me firmly at his mouth.

He deepened our kiss, thrusting his tongue into my mouth, sliding it over my teeth and then nipping at my lip. Instead of pulling my bottom lip between his, he pulled my top lip in, gently tugging it down and into his all-too-willing mouth. I groaned and let go of the bar. My hand grazed something else in his lap. Something that would probably fill me up a lot better than any type of food.

He pulled back, a smile playing on his lips. Then he reached between us, unwrapped one of the chocolate goodies, and held it up to my lips. I stared at him when I took a bite. I couldn't help the little groan that erupted when the chocolate hit my tongue and melted.

"Your little noises drive me insane," he murmured.

After I chewed and swallowed, he gestured for me to take another bite. "You have a thing for feeding me," I said as I chewed.

"A strong man always makes sure his woman is provided for. That she has everything she needs."

I paused in chewing, the food no longer holding my interest. "That sounds very possessive," I observed.

He smiled again. "I am a very possessive man, *bella*."

My stomach did a full three-sixty inside my body. I may not always know what direction I'm going, but I always make my own way. I'm not the type of girl who likes to be told what to do, who wants to be dictated to.

But Nash… he made being possessed sound like the most satisfying thing ever.

I grabbed the other bar and unwrapped. Then I held it up to his lips. "Eat."

He opened his mouth and bit into the food, his lips pulling away like it was a lollipop. We didn't say anything else. We just sat there and fed each other until the bars were gone.

And then he kissed me again, a lingering kiss that tasted like chocolate.

When I finally stood, I noticed that I had sand in places that weren't entirely comfortable. In fact, if I wasn't careful, it might turn painful. As I walked toward the water bottles, I moved a little funny, trying not to rub the sand farther into my, ummm… lady parts.

"*Bella*…" The little nickname he used more than my name sounded like an angry command. Then he was standing behind me, spinning me around, and

[118]

drilling his stare into mine. "Did I hurt you last night?"

"What? No!"

"You're walking funny. I tried to be gentle." His forehead creased.

I reached up and traced the cute lines.

"You were." I whispered. "It was... it was seriously the best experience of my life."

He relaxed, but the creases still didn't go away.

"I have sand in uncomfortable places," I admitted sheepishly.

He chuckled, the little lines disappearing. Before I knew what he was doing, he had my shower items in my messenger bag and he hoisted me up onto his back—piggyback style.

"Where are we going?" I asked, trying not to notice that when he walked, the muscles in his back moved and brushed against my crotch.

"To clean up," he said simply and then made his way deftly through the trees and plants while carrying me along.

Turns out ignoring any part of him was impossible.

By the time the little lagoon with the waterfall came into sight, I was practically panting with need.

Once again he seemed oblivious (really, are all men like this?) and sat me on my feet beside the water. "Take off your clothes," he said while unpacking the little bottles of shampoo and the bar of soap.

"Excuse me?" I replied, lifting an eyebrow.

He straightened, pinning me with those intense green eyes. He prowled—that's right, he didn't walk; *he prowled*—over in front of me and lifted the hem of the oversized shirt, his knuckles skimming the fronts of my thighs all the way up as he moved. "We need to get that sand off you, *bella*."

"Okay," I said dumbly as the shirt slid up over my arms and then fell to the ground, leaving me standing there in nothing but a little pair of panties. It wasn't cool outside, but the air felt chilled when it brushed over my fiery skin.

When he reached for the waistband of my panties, I jerked back. "Turn around," I ordered.

"You can't be serious."

"Oh, I'm serious." Last night had been dark, with nothing but the dying embers of the fire. This was broad daylight. What if he didn't like what he saw?

"I've seen every gorgeous inch of you."

"Turn. Around." If he said one more swoon-worthy thing, I was going to turn into his slave. I needed to reclaim some power.

He sighed and turned around. I ignored the way his shoulders shook with silent laughter and quickly peeled away the panties and waded into the water. When it was just past my hips, I froze. "Are there alligators in here?"

"Can I turn around now?" he asked.

"Yes!"

I glanced over my shoulder and around the curtain of hair that waved wildly about. "Alligators? Lochness Monster? Giant man-eating piranhas?" I said, suddenly about to panic.

He picked up something off the ground and walked into the water, shorts and all (how come I always end up naked and he got to keep his pants?) and wrapped his arms around me from behind. "I'll protect you."

Okay. I was lame. That totally made me feel better.

Nash took a few more steps into the water, forcing me along until we were chest deep. The sound of the waterfall hitting the lagoon was loud, but I didn't mind it. It was peaceful. And as it poured, little ripples played over the surface of the water to reach out and lap gently at us. The ends of my hair floated out, looking like a dark, golden halo.

Mist from the pouring falls drifted through the air, creating a translucent curtain around us and dampening all our skin that wasn't submerged in the water. I felt a moment's worry about getting my stitches damp with all the mist, but I stopped thinking about that the minute Nash spoke.

He wielded the bar of soap. "I'll wash you."
First he feeds me and then he washes me?
Sigh…

He lathered up his hands and started at the tops of my shoulders, smoothing the soap over my arms and neck and upper chest. Then he lifted my hands one by one and soaped from my elbow down. His hands slipped over my skin like velvet, like he was made of silk, and the lavender scent of the soap rose up around us and caught in the mist like a fly in a spider web.

When my upper body was clean, he used a hand to cup the water and pour it over my shoulders, rinsing away the bubbles.

And then there was nowhere to wash but down.

He used both his hands at once, closing over my breasts, groping them skillfully with soap-laden hands. Tiny tingles shot through me all the way down to my toes, and my head fell back because holding it up was just too much work.

The area between my legs began to throb, almost like it had a heartbeat of its own. His hands slid lower, over my abdomen, around my belly button, lower still.

"I'm getting closer to the sand, aren't I?" he murmured.

I moaned. My knees threatened to buckle.

Instead of continuing straight down, his hands separated and traveled around my hips. He stepped forward, bringing our chests together, and held me close while he washed my back, reaching up beneath my hair and sudsing up my neck. I leaned forward and pressed my lips to his shoulder, tempted to nip at his damp skin.

"Do it," he growled like he could read my mind.

Or maybe he just read my body.

I hesitated and he shifted, pressing closer. My lips opened automatically and my teeth sank lightly into his flesh. His hands spasmed and he pulled me roughly against him, my body—my very naked body—met with a very hard erection. It strained against the front of his shorts.

His hand slid over the round curve of my backside, slipping down lower… in between my legs, all from behind. He moved his fingers around like he was washing away the sand.

What he was really doing was turning me the hell on.

If I was throbbing before, I now felt like something down there was hammering with rabid force.

I whispered his name. It sounded more like a plea.

His fingers kept sliding, right up to that magic spot. I jerked a little because the jolt of pleasure was so intense. I bit him again. This time a little harder. His finger started to work me with a skill only he possessed... My body was ready to snap.

An approaching sound had us both stiffening. Nash released me and put his body in front of mine. "If I tell you to run, run," he said, effectively scaring me.

"I won't leave you," I whispered furiously.

He gave me a stern look over his shoulder. I ignored it.

The plants rustled; a few leaves and stems quivered with movement. I thought about the gunfire, the rhythm of the drums...

Nash's body tensed as someone stepped up to the water's edge.

12

It was Duke.

I wanted to pass out from relief.

He came up short when he noticed we were there. "Hey, I'm sorry. I didn't realize you were here."

I peaked around Nash's shoulder. "No worries. We were just cleaning up a little."

He nodded, his eyes going straight to me. They seemed strained. It made me feel a little guilty. I'm not sure why.

Nash glanced over his shoulder, looking at me, and then walked onto shore. His shorts were soaked and the weight of the water pulled at them, making them ride incredibly low on his hips.

I tried not to stare... and I failed.

"You're dressed," Duke observed, his voice a little more than relieved.

"Ava is a little less covered," Nash said tightly. "Turn around."

Duke immediately turned around, and for some reason I found his eager respect for me endearing.

Nash dug into the messenger bag and pulled out one of his T-shirts. The one I'd been using as a towel. I hurried closer, my hair doing a good job of covering my breasts. Nash wrapped the shirt around me as I wrung some of the moisture out of the ends of my hair and then pinned him with a stare as well.

He gave an exaggerated sigh and turned around as well.

When I was sure they weren't peeking, I quickly put on my panties and T-shirt again. Then I packed up the soap and slung the wet shirt over my shoulder. "You both can turn around now."

They both paused, then turned. I smiled sheepishly. "Thanks."

Nash reached out and took the bag from me.

"Wanna hang out with us?" I asked Duke.

"Sure."

The three of us went back to the plane, the wet tips of my hair a tangled mess around my shoulders. Nash came inside the plane as I was taming the beast that was my hair and grabbed up a couple coconuts and went outside to open them.

Duke hovered at the back opening of the plane. "Come in," I called out. "There's some water right there." I gestured to the bottles. "And fruit if you want some."

He grabbed a mango off the pile and then moved around, looking at the wrecked plane. "That was some landing, huh?"

"I'll say," I agreed as I braided my hair down over my shoulder.

"I've never been on a plane before," he said, still gazing around with interest.

"Really?"

Cambria Hebert

"I always traveled by boat." His hair was waving around his face, not tucked behind his ears today. It looked soft and it still flipped up at the ends.

"Wanna see the cockpit?"

"Yeah." He followed me into the front of the plane with the large windows and the controls. It was messier up here because we didn't bother to clean up as much, knowing this part of the plane wouldn't get much use.

"Wow," he murmured, sitting down in the pilot's seat. "Look at all these controls." He pointed at one. "Wonder what this one did."

I couldn't see so I stepped forward, and my clumsy butt tripped over the crap on the floor and I fell forward.

Right into Duke's lap.

"If you wanted to drive, you should have just said so," he quipped.

I couldn't help it; I laughed.

To my surprise, he settled me into his lap, both of us facing the window, and looped his arms around my waist.

"Do you miss home?" I asked him softly.

"Every day."

"Have you tried to get off the island?"

"More times than I could count."

"Maybe with three of us, it will be easier. Maybe we can figure something out."

"Maybe," he said. He leaned his forehead against the back of my shoulder.

"We will." I corrected him. "You, me, and Nash."

"Are you two together?"

"What do you mean?" I asked, even though I knew what he meant. I had no idea how to respond to that. The answer was no, Nash and I weren't together.

A strong man always makes sure his woman is provided for.

But we weren't exactly not not together either...

I think I just confused myself.

"I mean, like, is he your man?"

Was he? I opened my mouth, interested in what was going to come out, but I never got the chance to see.

Nash chose that moment to walk in. His eyes went right to me... in Duke's lap. It was completely innocent... but I wasn't sure he saw it that way.

He stalked over and held out a coconut to me. I started to stand to take it and tripped again. Nash's hands were full. But Duke's weren't. He caught me and eased me up on my feet, his hands lingering on my waist. "Careful," he murmured as he pulled away.

"Here," Nash said, handing the second coconut to Duke.

"Thank you," he said, accepting it.

Nash reached for my arm and held me steady as I walked through the debris and out of the cockpit. Then he handed me the last coconut. "What about you?" I asked, frowning.

"I'll open another one," he said, turning his back and going to do just that. I stared after him, feeling like I should have said something... but I didn't know what he wanted me to say.

"Let's go down to the beach," I said to Duke.

When he stood, I couldn't help but notice his gaze lingering on my legs. I realized then that my long shirt made it look like I wasn't wearing pants.

Crap. I wasn't.

"Would you mind holding this outside while I change?"

He took it and disappeared. Quickly, I yanked off the shirt and pulled on my bikini and a yellow cotton sundress I had in my suitcase. It made a good cover-up.

Duke was waiting for me beside the plane, and when I came to the edge, he moved forward to help me down. He glanced down at his full hands and scowled.

"It's okay." I laughed. "I jump down all the time."

He shook his head, but I didn't give him time to react and try and help me. I jumped down, landing lightly beside him. The last thing I wanted was for Nash to happen to see Duke with his hands on me again, helping me down.

"Let's go down to the beach," Nash suggested from somewhere beside the plane. His voice was close by and I felt some relief knowing that my decision to avoid Duke's touch was a good one.

I tried not to think about why I cared so much what Nash thought.

The three of us wandered down to the sand. My eyes went right to the bonfire pit and my cheeks heated with the memory of what we did there last night. Nash caught my eye and I knew he was thinking the same thing by the way his gaze traveled my body. His stare felt like a laser beam, retracing the path his tongue had made just hours before.

We all sat quiet for a moment as we drank the sweet juice from the fruit. My thoughts turned to the gunshots we heard and the warning Duke gave us just before he left.

"We heard gunfire last night," I said. I didn't bother looking at Nash. I knew he wasn't keen on asking Duke about what we'd been hearing, but I didn't care anymore. We were stuck here, like it or not. We needed to know what we were dealing with.

Duke nodded. "It's on the other side of the island."

"Have you been there? Are there people? Civilization?" Hope swarmed up inside me like a tidal wave, thinking this could be our way off this island, that this could help us get home.

"It's not safe to go there," Duke said tightly.

"Why not?"

He pinned me with his dark eyes. "It just isn't. You won't find help there. Stay on this side."

"But won't they come here eventually?"

Duke just gazed off across the ocean, almost like he was lost in thought. Or wistful for home.

"You okay?" I asked him, reaching out and laying a hand on his arm. He looked down, almost like he was startled by the contact.

His eyes slid to mine. "Yeah, I'm good." So much emotion swam in those eyes of his. They had to be the most expressive I had ever seen.

We sat there frozen for long moments, my hand on his arm and his eyes memorizing every angle of my face (at least that's what it felt like).

"You gonna tell us what's out there or what?" Nash said.

I gave him a hard look because he was being rude. He should be nice. This poor guy didn't have anyone. For months.

Duke hesitated.

Nash sighed and stood, sand sticking to his still-damp shorts. "If you won't tell me, I'm damn sure going to find out."

"What does that mean?" I asked, alarmed.

"It means we're going to the other side of the island. We're going hunting."

13

"Are you sure this is a good idea?" I asked for the hundredth time since we started walking.

Nash stopped suddenly, and I bumped into his back, stumbling backward a bit. He turned swiftly and glanced at me. "I don't know what else to do," he said grimly. "Do I want to walk into potential dangerous territory... with you right behind me? No. I don't. But being a sitting duck isn't safe either. I'd rather know what we're dealing with."

I glanced at Duke, who was standing there watching us. "Can't you just tell us what's there?"

"I already told you it was no good. I told you to stay away."

"You won't tell us why?" I implored.

"Because it is," was his simple reply.

Nash made a sound and started walking again. "If it's so dangerous, why are you coming with us?" he tossed over his shoulder.

Duke didn't reply, but I felt his stare and I turned to look at him. It was because of me. He was coming along because of me. I glanced at Nash to see if he realized, but he hadn't turned around. He was to intent on our path.

We walked in silence after that, forever it seemed. My feet grew tired and my body was damp with sweat. I was so not the camping/hiking kind of girl. And to make it worse, I kept thinking about the dream. About the two men who were right beside me.

Every so often I would feel Duke's eyes and I would look at him. He had this way of gazing at me… this sort of longing in his eyes… It made me feel coveted. It made me feel wanted.

But then I would look at Nash, at the way his hips swiveled when he walked. The way his shoulder muscles moved beneath all that olive-toned skin. And his hands were magic. But beyond that… he seemed to care about me, like he thought of me first, even before himself.

I tried to direct my thoughts away from my company and pay attention to the surroundings. The island was lush and beautiful. The greenery was everywhere. Palm trees and tall plants full of colorful, blossoming flowers filled the air with a heady scent. Because we were close to the ocean, there was still a bit of a breeze, even this far into the island.

Still, it wasn't as cool as it was right on the sand because the trees and plants kind of worked as a trap for the heat, keeping it in instead of letting it drift up and away. At least the sunlight didn't shine directly on us. I wasn't sure if my fair skin could take the brutal midday rays. So far I had been lucky to avoid a sunburn, but I knew it was probably only a matter of time.

I started to feel lightheaded when we stepped into a particularly cool part of the wilderness. The trees were heavier here so the shade was denser. It felt wonderful against my heated skin, but it also seemed to serve as a reminder of just how hot I actually was.

My thoughts grew thick and it felt weird to walk, my legs feeling like Jell-O.

"Do you think we could stop for a minute?" I asked. "Take a break?"

Both Duke and Nash came to my side, Nash reaching me first. "Of course." He studied me. "Your skin is flushed."

"I'm just really hot."

He led me over beneath a tree where the leaves were bigger than my head. We sat down below it, leaning up against the trunk.

"Here," Duke said, handing me his untouched bottle of water. I have no idea how he hadn't drank any. My bottle was already gone.

He must have seen my shock when he handed me the full bottle because he said, "I've gotten used to this heat."

"But you might need it," I protested.

"You need it more," he said, giving my hand a squeeze. Then he turned thoughtful. "I think there's some fruit around here. I'm going to grab some. You should eat something."

"You shouldn't be alone." I worried. "Nash can go with you."

"I'm not leaving you alone," Nash said instantly.

Duke nodded. "He should stay. I won't be long."

When I frowned, he offered me a smile. "I promise I'll be okay."

I nodded and within moments he disappeared behind a beautiful plant with bright-pink blooms.

"I don't trust him," Nash said.

"Why?"

"Just a feeling I get."

"But he's helped us. He showed us food. He gave us that machete."

"I don't like the way he looks at you."

"I'm tired," I said, leaning my head against the tree. I didn't really want to talk about Duke with Nash. I sort of felt like I was caught between them.

He brushed a few damp strands of hair off my cheek. "Just sit here and cool off. Rest."

It didn't take long for my eyes to grow heavy and begin to drift closed...

I felt the blanket drift down over my chilled skin. It wasn't warm like he was, but I knew that soon it would trap the heat the night air was leeching from my body and give it back to me. I sighed, settling in a little farther.

My comfort was slightly interrupted when I realized I was still on the beach, still lying in the sand. I turned my head and glanced at the bonfire, which had grown cold. The glowing embers had long gone out.

It was just me, the glittering stars overhead, and the sound of the waves crashing harmoniously against the shore.

But something was missing.

No.

Someone was missing.

Just as I thought to lift my head, to call out for him, I felt a gentle caress brush my ankle. A little of the ocean air drifted beneath the blanket as his hand traveled farther up, caressing my calf and making me smile. I lay still, not wanting him to stop, wondering where his curious hand would lead him.

Farther up he traveled until his palm was brushing over the outside of my thigh, stroking the skin, coaxing my body to turn for him.

It did. With a soft sigh I rolled onto my back, opening my eyes just enough so I could stare up at the stars.

Starlight, star bright,
First star I see tonight,
I wish I may, I wish I might,
Have this boy I want tonight.

And oh how I wished for him.

The universe heard my plea, and I watched as a shooting star dripped from the heavens, streaking the sky with a glimmering trail.

His fingers kept exploring, slipping beneath my shorts, hovering over my bikini bottoms, and brushing against my core. My hips tilted upward automatically, inviting his touch.

He was like a drug. An addiction. His fingers were my dealer and his lips were my poison. I lived for my next fix, the next time his knuckles would graze the softness of my inner thigh, the next time he would gently scrape his fingernails across my lower abdomen and then delve into my soft curls at the apex of my hips.

I moaned softly when he dipped beneath my bottoms, his skin touching my skin. I was already wet for him, and I felt my moisture coat his fingers as he slipped along my entrance.

He moved closer, his body settling between my spread legs and his free hand reaching up to cup my breast, to squeeze it lightly and roll the hardened nipple between his finger.

"Nash," I whispered, arching into him, practically begging for more.

I had no idea that my body could ever feel this way. That I would ever need another person's touch so much. That if I didn't get it, I might slowly go insane. It was like he started a clock the first time he touched me, a ticking clock on a bomb that counted the minutes, the seconds until the time ran out and I exploded in a heap of desire.

He stilled, his fingers pausing in their perusal, and I felt his stare through the dark. I started to sit up, but he pressed me back down, his fingers scissoring open, testing me, stretching me.

My breathing turned ragged; my body hummed. Now. I wanted him now. I grabbed his wrist and pulled him up over me, blocking out the stars with his dark shape.

He was completely shrouded in darkness. I couldn't see his face at all.

Something like hesitation creeped over me. My body tried to deny it, to push it away and hang on to its need.

"Nash?" I whispered, staring above me.

Slowly he shook his head…

I jerked awake. Sweat slicked my skin and my heart pounded erratically. That was the most vivid dream I ever experienced. Not to mention the sexiest one.

"Hey," Nash said from right beside me. "You having another nightmare—about the crash?"

"Did I fall asleep?" I asked, looking up at him.

"You were tired," he said gently, tracing a finger beneath my eyes where I was sure dark circles resided.

"I never sleep in the middle of the day," I said, frowning.

And I never have sex dreams about strangers, either.

"You've never been a victim of a plane crash, out in the heat all day, traipsing over an unknown island, and practically dehydrated, either." Then he glanced at me. "Have you?"

That elicited a giggle. "Are you kidding? This is like my hobby."

He snorted.

I couldn't help but notice the way we were sitting. Side by side, but I might as well have been in his lap. My leg was firmly pressed along his and my upper body was leaning into him, draped over his chest. His arm was around my waist, securing me close, and I knew that my head likely was resting on his shoulder.

"You drool," he said, offering me a grin.

I smacked him. "I do not!"

"Maybe you weren't having a nightmare. Maybe you were dreaming about me." He wagged his eyebrows.

My stomach lurched.

He frowned. "Hey, you feeling okay?" he asked, concern totally eclipsing his playful tone from just seconds ago.

"I'm fine," I said, sitting up, pushing away from him.

"Here," he said, uncapping a bottle of water and holding it out. I took it and drank a few gulps.

The water was warm, but I didn't care. It was wet.

Wet. Oh God, between my legs was wet. That dream had really turned me on.

Why would I dream that? What was wrong with my body? We were off on a hunt for who knows what, and I was falling asleep and having naughty dreams like we really were on vacation.

"Ava," Nash said. He took my hand and I glanced at him.

Man, I loved his hair. All messy, unruly curls that caught in the breeze and moved around his head like they just wanted to flirt with me.

It's just him, I told myself. I'd never been this turned on, this amped up sexually before. After what happened last night by the fire, it was only natural that I would dream like that, considering the fact that every time he looked at me since, all I wanted to do was finish what we started.

Get a grip, Ava! I yelled at myself. Geesh, I was like a guy, thinking about sex twenty-four-seven.

Once again, my brain didn't seem to get the memo. A vision of the man over me in the dream floated behind my eyes. I concentrated hard, looking for the outline of those curls in the dark.

I tried to think about the way he smelled, if the scent was familiar, like the natural scent Nash carried.

There wasn't anything. Not an inkling of a clue. But it had to be him. No one, and I mean no one, ever affected me the way he does.

Besides, who else could it be?

Duke stepped around a tree, his eyes going straight to me. He smiled and my stomach did a little somersault. Okay, it didn't do a little somersault. It did one of those ungraceful belly flops that have people wincing in pain as they watch you smack into the water with a sharp slapping sound.

Oh no.

Duke came closer and sat down on the other side of me, effectively making me into a man sandwich. I laughed at little beneath my breath. Ava was a man-wich.

I was completely losing it.

"I found some fruit," Duke said, holding out some fresh mangos and an avocado.

"Thank you," I said, reaching for the mango.

Nash made a sound and reached around me. "No. Eat the avocado. I think you need something a little more substantial right now."

Did he know I was losing it too?

"Clearly your body is running really low on fuel." He continued. "It's why you're so tired."

Was that all it was? Low blood sugar?

When I glanced back at Duke, he'd managed to split open the avocado, exposing the light green and ripened flesh.

"Thank you."

I threw myself into eating. And I avoided the stares from the man-wich. It was easier to eat than think right then.

Probably because my thoughts were very disturbing.

That dream... If it hadn't been Nash... there was only one other person it could be.

I glanced back up, my eyes instantly colliding with Duke's.

Could it have been him?

14

It was easy to realize when we got close to the other side of the island. Duke grew quiet, even stoic. So much so that I fell back a little and matched my steps with his, walking at his side.

He glanced at me and I offered him a small smile.

He reached out and threaded our hands together, holding tightly to me. I didn't pull away. I couldn't. I realized I needed the reassurance just as much as he seemed to.

Up ahead the trees seemed to part, giving way to the beach, and I could hear the waves crashing onto the shore just ahead. We all slowed, creeping to the side and behind a large fern, ducking behind the leaves.

Nash turned to look at me, his eyes going right to me.

Duke joined our hands. He didn't say anything, but the skin around his mouth tightened.

"I'm going to go closer," Nash whispered. "Stay here."

"Wait," I whisper-yelled.

He turned back. "If you hear gunshots, run. Run and don't look back."

That was probably the scariest thing I ever heard in my entire life. The idea of Nash being shot. The idea of me running away and leaving him behind.

The thought of never seeing him again.

He didn't give me a chance to protest. When he disappeared, my stomach began to churn violently. The avocado I ate earlier threatened to make a second appearance. Even though the food did make me feel better, I shouldn't have eaten it. I should have pretended I was too weak to continue and then Nash would have taken me back to the plane. We wouldn't be here right now... He wouldn't be out there...

I jumped when he reappeared, his eyes a little wider, a little darker than before. I stood, ripping my hand out of Duke's and rushing forward. I threw myself at him, but he was ready. He caught me, folding me close and burying his face in my hair. I could feel the pounding of his heart against my chest and I knew that he had been afraid.

"What is it?" I whispered, pulling back and searching his eyes.

"There are definitely other people on this island."

"Did you see them?" I asked excitedly, thinking this might be our lucky day.

"No," Nash said, and I noticed he wasn't as excited.

"What aren't you telling me?"

He looked past me at Duke. "You knew, didn't you?"

He only nodded.

"Knew what?" I demanded, not enjoying being the only one who didn't know what was going on.

"These people won't help us," Nash answered, his eyes never leaving Duke.

"What people!" I demanded, my voice a little louder. Nash placed a couple fingers to my lips.

"Pirata," he whispered.

Like I knew what that meant. After days of listening to him randomly speak Spanish, it still sounded like a bunch of gibberish. I wanted to shake him and say, "Use your words, man!" but I decided that probably wouldn't be a good idea, so I gave him an exasperated look instead.

"Come on," he said, taking my hand. "I'll show you."

The three of us moved out of the cover of trees and onto the beach. This side of the beach was a little different than our side. It was a little rougher here; there were some rocks around the shore, some of them jutting out into the ocean. Against the rocks sat what appeared to be a little one-room cabin—well, more like a shack.

The wood was all weathered and gray; the roof was uneven and flat. There was one window, but it didn't have glass. There was a piece of what looked like tin rested beneath it, and I had the idea that whoever lived there just placed the tin in the window when it rained.

There were no steps leading into the crooked, warped front door. The shack just sat right there in the sand.

I wasn't curious at all what was inside.

In fact, the idea of going in there at all gave me a serious case of heebie-jeebies.

The pristine white sand was cluttered here— littered with empty barrels and a long wooden table with more barrels shoved beneath as stools. Beside the table was a chest and I wandered over and lifted the lid. Inside were playing cards and poker chips. There were cigarettes and cigars. I pocketed one of the many lighters, thinking it might come in handy if we ever needed to start a fire quickly.

There were empty beer bottles all over the place, some of them rolling around in the surf. Fishing nets were strung among some of the barrels and a bar ran across the middle of a large fire pit. I assumed it was used to hang fish from to roast.

I wandered a little closer to the surf, toward the rocks and away from that creepy shack. Something on the rocks caught my attention and I jogged to it, looking at the chains that literally hung from the jagged rock.

My stomach churned again. Why would someone have chains like this? A smear of something dark against the rocks gave me the answer and made me gag. Blood.

Obviously, these chains weren't here for fun and games.

I left the chains, my overactive imagination not needing to see any more, and something on the water caught my eye. I ran around to the side and saw it, sitting out in the open right there on the other side of the rocks.

A boat.

Not just one boat.

Many boats.

I turned, seeking out Nash and Duke. They weren't far, and I waved my arms at them, trying to get their attention without yelling.

Duke saw me first and came jogging forward. I saw Nash shove something in his pants and then look up. I waved to him and he ran over, his eyes searching the area all around me.

"Look," I said excitedly when they were both within hearing distance. I pointed to the boats.

Nash let out a whoop of joy and picked me up, spinning me around. I grinned. Finally, a way off this island. "We even have a sailor right here to sail us to safety!" I said, touching Duke on the arm.

He gave me a warm smile, but not before sadness passed behind his eyes.

"Let's go," Nash said, and the three of started toward the boats.

As we got closer, it became clear that something wasn't quite right.

From where we stood before, the boats appeared heaven sent, like a beacon, a sign of home and safety.

From up close... They were a disappointment.

The first boat we came too was nothing but a mere shell. The engine, the steering wheel, and everything that would make the boat actually run were stripped away.

Nash climbed onto the boat and it sagged down into the waves dangerously low. He let out a curse and climbed out. "There's a hole in it."

I stepped forward and sure enough, just his weight caused the boat to take on water.

I ran to the one not too far away. It was on the shore, the waves barely reaching it. It was stripped of parts just like the other one. This one had tarps and rope inside.

We started checking all of them, refusing to give up hope, praying that just one would be suitable to sail.

But none of them were.

All hope inside me died.

The kind of death suitable to a graveyard.

A boat graveyard.

"Some of these boats were once really nice," Nash said, looking at them all grimly.

"Not anymore," I intoned and set back in the direction we came. Maybe we should search the creepy shack. Maybe there was a phone or something inside.

But that's when I saw it.

Another boat. A ship actually. A large white one that cut through the water like a warm knife in butter. It was so pristine it actually gleamed in the sunlight. There was a large flag billowing with the wind, but I couldn't tell what was on it. The boat was still too far away.

But not for long.

It was headed in this direction.

I called to Nash and Duke and they saw it too. Nash rushed to my side and pulled me down behind the rocks, keeping us from sight. Every few moments, he or Duke would peek over, looking to see what was happening.

I looked back at the boats, the ones that had been practically vandalized and left there to be used as storage. I thought about the creepy shack, the poker chips… the blood and the chains.

Whoever lived here was home.

Whoever lived here was not going to help us.

Nash's whispered Spanish word drifted through my head. *Pirata.*

I didn't have to ask him to tell me what it meant. I knew.

Pirates.

15

It took half the time to get back to our side of the island than it did to get across to the pirates'. Adrenaline and fear are great motivators. Not to mention that once Nash thought we were far enough away from the pirates not to be heard, he set a punishing pace.

Twice, I thought my lungs were going to burst (from being scared silly or being out of breath, I couldn't tell), but thankfully, Duke was there to spur me on and give me a hand. At one point, I was pretty sure he actually picked me up and ran with me.

It wasn't embarrassing at all. (*Not.*)

I decided then that when I got home—*if* I got home—running was going to be my new hobby.

When we reached the little lagoon with the wide waterfall, Nash finally stopped and I doubled over, clutching my middle and sucking in lungfuls of air.

I felt a large hand settle on my back and rub slow circles. "Just breathe," a voice instructed. I looked up.

It was Duke.

"We… should… have… listened…" I wheezed.

"Sometimes you have to see something for yourself to believe it," he said kindly.

Nash thrust a newly filled bottle of water under my nose. "Drink," he said, not even sounding out of breath. It made me want to kick him in the shin. I mean, he had fabulous hair, a year-round tan, was a pilot, *and* he was Mr. Fitness? The boy was beyond blessed.

I took the water and gulped it down, choking as it caught in my throat. I started hacking as tears blurred my vision. I thrust the water away from me and Duke took it as my body continued to make a fool of itself.

Nash's hand cupped the back of my neck and he brought his face close to mine, holding it still as coughs still wracked my chest. "Easy, *bella*," he whispered. He was so close that his lips practically brushed mine.

My breath caught.

The coughing stopped.

He kneaded the muscles in my neck lightly, easing some of the tension coiled in my body. "There you go," he murmured when I was breathing calmly.

"Do you think they saw us?" I worried and then glanced at Duke. "Or heard us?"

He shook his head. "They'd be chasing us."

I bit my lip, still worrying. "I thought pirates were only made up for movies and TV."

"I've hear the rumors of modern-day pirates," Nash said grimly. "First time I've seen one."

"What do they do?" I wondered out loud. My knowledge of pirates was limited to Captain Hook from *Peter Pan* and Johnny Depp from *Pirates of the*

Caribbean. Something told me that these "modern-day" pirates weren't the same.

I noticed that neither man was rushing to explain. Well, that couldn't be good.

I glanced at Duke. "What do they do?"

He seemed sad to have to tell me about such things. "Oceans don't usually fall under regular jurisdiction laws of our government. Meaning it's basically a free-for-all out there. Pirates sail the seas, take over boats, rob people, and take hostages."

"Hostages!" I cried. "What on Earth for?"

Neither one of them answered.

I made a frustrated sound. "I'm not a two-year-old!" I snapped.

"They also murder people," Duke said grimly.

"Murder?" I echoed.

"Yes, *bella*, money is a very powerful motive to kill."

"They live on this island—on that side—because it's unchartered. Because no one would look for them there. They literally commit their crimes and then come back here to hide," Duke told us.

"It's the perfect setup," I whispered, totally appalled.

"We need to get off this island," Nash said.

"If only one of those boats had been salvageable, we could sail away."

We fell into silence, but it wasn't particularly comfortable. It was more ominous. I kind of wished we didn't know what was over there. Then I wouldn't be so scared.

I sat down by the water's edge and plunged my feet into the cool liquid. It felt so good against my flushed skin. All that running had made my legs shaky and my body overheated. I stared out at the water, thinking about going for a swim to cool off.

Then I thought about this morning when I was in the water... with Nash.

I shook my head, disgusted with myself. How could I think about sex when murdering pirates were on the loose? Clearly my priorities were not what they should be. I glanced over my shoulder at Nash. He looked back, spearing me with a heated look.

Clearly his priorities weren't that great either.

But, in our defense, thinking about sex was a lot better than thinking about most everything else.

Nash looked away. "Can you stay with her?" he asked Duke.

"Of course."

I was about to argue about not needing a babysitter, but I stopped. I didn't want to be left alone now. Even if I happened upon a Johnny Depp/Captain Jack Sparrow lookalike, I would run away screaming (and we already know how horrible I am at running; I might as well be a turtle trying to run in a puddle of peanut butter).

"Where are you going?" I asked nervously.

"I'm going to check the plane, make sure no one found it."

"You shouldn't go alone," I said, starting to rise.

"You're not coming," he said, his voice hard and unforgiving.

Geesh, rude much?

Duke sat down beside me, his feet joining mine in the water, as Nash disappeared. I sighed. "Hey, there aren't any man-eating piranha's in here, are there?"

"If we see one, I'll catch it for dinner," he said and then winked.

I laughed.

"What's the best thing about being here?" I asked.

"Meeting you."

I actually blushed. "I *am* the prettiest girl on the island," I said confidently. Never mind I was likely the *only* girl on the island.

"Most definitely."

"What's the worst thing about being here?"

"Wanting to go home."

"Hey," I said softly, reaching out to place my hand over his. "We will get home."

He smiled sadly. I guess for a guy who's been trapped here for so long, hope didn't come as easy to him as it did to me.

He didn't say anything else. Instead, he flipped my hand over and studied my palm, moving his finger in slow circles over my skin. Little butterflies fluttered softly in my belly, and the water gently swooshed against my ankles as I moved my feet back and forth.

"Want to go swimming?" I asked, trying to lighten the mood. It bothered me to see him this way. I wanted to see him smile. I wanted him to be happy.

The corner of his lip pulled up. "Sure."

I stood and tossed my yellow dress onto the shore, then jumped into the water and paddled around. "Come on!" I called.

Seconds later, Duke jumped in—fully clothed—and met me in the center in just a few graceful strokes. He swam so skillfully he barely made any ripples in the surface of the water. "You're a good swimmer."

"I've always loved the water."

"Is that why you became a sailor?"

"Yeah."

He ducked under the water and then popped back up, shaking his head like a dog and spraying me with water droplets. I laughed and splashed him back. He growled and I squealed, lunging away, farther into the water.

He gave chase, but I knew that he was letting me get away. Because he was such a strong swimmer, he would have caught me easily if he wanted to.

It didn't take long for me to get tired (clearly, athletics are *not* my strong suit), and I slowed down, treading water near the tumbling waterfall. From this angle, it looked like it fell right from the sky and plunged into the water, creating bubbles and a thin layer of white foam over the surface.

"You ever been on the inside of a waterfall?" Duke whispered from right behind me.

"No."

"Come on," he said and pushed away, swimming right through the curtain of water.

I followed, a little surprised that the water falling down was colder than the water we were swimming in. Behind the falls was almost like a secret cove. The lighting was much dimmer here, the ripples in the surface reflecting off the smooth rock walls inside. Moss grew over some of the surfaces here, softening the rock and giving everything the feel of a secret garden.

The sound of the falling water wasn't as loud back here as I thought it would be. It was like this little cove muffled the sound, kept too much from coming in so it could be a perfect spot for resting.

Duke was sitting on a rock, staring at the curtain of water. I swam over and he held out a hand, hoisting me up onto the slippery rock. "It's pretty back here."

"Yeah," he said. "I come here a lot to think."

"I can see why."

"I used to wish I had someone sitting here to share it with." He looked over at me, his eyes like a chocolate molten cake, warm from the oven. "And here you are."

"Here I am," I declared, unable to look away.

His gaze was hungry, like he might devour me in two bites, but those two bites would be worth it because I would be the absolute best thing he ever tasted.

A drop of water rolled over my forehead, into the corner of my eye, and fell, like a single tear down my cheek. Duke captured it with his thumb and pulled it away, placing the same thumb into his mouth.

My eyes zeroed in on that thumb and the way his tongue caressed it, the way his lips sucked it. He pulled the thumb out and ran it over my lower lip; it was slightly moist from his saliva.

My heart thudded as he closed the distance between us.

His lips brushed over mine, a brief and gentle stroke. Then he pulled back and looked at me. His eyes were swimming with desire, swimming with all kinds of longing and wonder.

He moved to kiss me again; this time I knew it would be deeper. This time I knew he would want to kiss me until our lungs seized and the need for oxygen pulled us apart.

I couldn't.

"Ava!" someone yelled from the other side of the falls.

I jerked away from Duke as I heard a muffled curse, and then he yelled again. "Ava!"

It was Nash. And he was worried.

I scrambled up, nearly slipping, and rushed to the side of the waterfall. I leaned out, balancing against the rock. "Nash!" I called.

He turned swiftly when I called, his entire body sagging with relief. He ran a hand through his hair, and his chest heaved. Then he dove way out into the water, swimming toward the waterfall with great purpose.

I sat back down beside Duke just as Nash popped up, giving his head a toss and wiping the water out of his eyes. "Cool place," he said, looking around.

Duke cleared his throat. "I should probably go, make sure my camp is still okay."

"You should stay with us," I told him again. I'd offered many times, but he never agreed. "It would be safer if we all stayed together."

"I'll be fine."

I caught his arm. "Think about it," I implored.

His eyes softened. "I will."

"See you in the morning?"

He smiled. "I'll bring you a coconut."

"Yum."

He walked to the edge of the rock and lifted his arms over his head, preparing to dive. His wet shirt rode up, exposing a small portion of his lower back.

And the end of a thick scar.

I stared at it, wondering if the reason he didn't walk around shirtless like Nash was because he was trying to keep something covered. As I pondered that, he jumped into the water and swam away.

Nash climbed onto the rock, taking Duke's spot. "He kissed you, didn't he?"

If there was any question that could pull my thoughts away from what I was thinking, it was that. I made a sound. "Why would you think that?"

"Because if I was him, I would have brought you back here to kiss you."

I snorted but otherwise didn't reply.

"Did you kiss him back?" he asked, all trace of arrogance and playfulness gone.

"No," I whispered. "You interrupted."

He grinned. "I've got damn good timing."

He jumped into the water, swimming toward the falling water. Then he turned back. "You're welcome, by the way."

"And what do you think I need to thank you for?"

"It would have been all kinds of awkward for him when you didn't kiss him back."

"Who says I wouldn't have kissed him back?" I countered, lifting an eyebrow.

A few strokes and he was beside the rock. He reached up and wrapped his hand around my ankle and slowly towed me forward. I slid right into the water, but before I could plunge into its depths, he pinned me with his body. My back arched against the rock and he leaned in close.

"Because he isn't me."

A shiver started at my feet and worked its way all the way up. He looked smug.

"I'm cold." I lied.

"Are you?" he whispered, coming close—so close that I could feel his warm breath fan across my lips. My tongue jetted out, moistening them, waiting for his kiss.

He didn't kiss me.

He swam away. "We better go, then."

I stared daggers at the back of his head and his laughter echoed around the cove. He was standing on the shore when I swam up, and he helped me up, reaching down and scooping up my dress.

"I want to show you something," he said, taking my hand.

He led us onto the darkened beach, walking across the sand, past the place where we had a bonfire. I didn't pay attention to how far we walked because I was completely distracted by the moon.

It was perfectly round, huge, and the color of a russet sunset. It was absolutely stunning. The kind of sight that made me wish I had a camera because I knew I would never see it quite this beautiful again.

It was still rising, sitting just above the water, and it was so large and produced so much light I finally understood the term "a moonlit night." I never really got it at home. Yes, the moon came out, but it was never really bright enough to light the dark. Until now.

"I've never seen a more beautiful moon," I told him as we walked.

"Me either."

I could stare at it all night. I wanted to commit it to memory, to never forget just how incredible it was.

A little while later, he pulled me closer to the trees and I looked at him, puzzled.

"I have something for you," he said, pulling me around so the only place I could look was his beautiful moonlit face.

"What is it?"

"I thought you deserved something special after the day we had."

I melted a little at his words, though it wasn't really his words. It was the consideration behind them. The fact that he thought of me enough to want to make a craptastic day just a little bit better.

Curiosity pulled at me and I smiled.

"Ready?" he asked softly, grasping me by the shoulders.

I nodded, squeezing my eyes shut with anticipation. He spun me around.

I opened my eyes and looked.

16

It was swaying lightly in the breeze and was big enough for two.

I smiled. "Where in the world did you find a hammock?"

"The other side of the island."

I bit my lip. "Do you think they will notice it's gone?"

He shook his head. "It was in that boat with all the rope and the tarps. It was buried at the bottom."

"I love it." Now we really could stare at the moon all night. "When did you do this?"

"When you were in the cove, kissing Duke." He teased.

But it wasn't a joke, not to me. "Nash," I whispered, touching his cheek. Trying to find the words. I wasn't even sure what I wanted to say.

"I was only kidding, *bella*," he soothed, pulling me closer. Both of us were still slightly damp from the water. "I know he's interested. I can see it every time he looks at you."

"Are you jealous?"

He shook his head. "No."

"No?"

"He's jealous of me."

"And why is that?" I murmured, looping my hands around his neck and playing with the ends of his hair.

"Because I'm the one with you right now. I'm the one who's going to steal away your heart."

"Confident," I replied, trying to play it cool, even though deep down inside I was sweltering. My heart was definitely considering a leap into his hands.

"Not confident," he murmured, finally brushing a kiss across my lips. "Certain."

I let him have the last say. I was done bantering. I wanted his lips upon mine. He gave me a deep kiss, his tongue massaging against mine, and then he pulled me backward toward the hammock.

He was the first one in, leaving one foot firmly planted on the ground as he opened his arms up to me, inviting me into the little swing. I snuggled up along his side and he lifted his leg, wrapping it around my legs and setting the hammock to a gentle swaying motion.

I sighed as the cool ocean air flirted with my skin, the sound of the surf lulled my body into a boneless position, and the moon stood watch over the night.

Nash played with my hair, pulling his fingers through it all the way until they cleared the long strands, and then he would start all over again. I curled my fingers into his chest, snuggling as close as I could against him. If I could have found a way inside him, I would already be there.

Eventually his hands drifted away from my hair and traveled down my body, grazing the side of my breast. I was already wound tight, still worked up from the night before, and I groaned, arching into his hand farther.

"You like that?" he murmured, stroking me again.

"Mmmm."

The next thing I knew, my top was gone and I was lying flat against the hammock as he stared down at me with passion-laden eyes. He kissed me deeply, his tongue taking over the inside of my mouth. I was completely breathless when he pulled away, his lips closing over my puckered nipple and gently sucking at it while he made tiny growling sounds that vibrated my entire breast.

I grabbed his head, holding it to me, not wanting him to stop, needing more of his lavishing attention. He moved on to the other breast, stopping in the hollow between them, licking the skin and then blowing on the wet flesh. I shuddered and began to writhe below him.

He rocked his hips forward and I felt the rock-hard length of him. Immediately, I spread my legs, wrapping them around his waist and locking him into position.

The hammock swayed as we dry-humped each other until I literally ached with need. When he pulled back, my entire body was shaking, shaking so badly that my teeth were chattering.

"Are you cold, *bella*?" he asked, concerned.

"No." I reached up to the button on his shorts. "We were interrupted last night," I said, releasing the closure.

"We were."

"I still want to see you."

We moved so he was lying on his back and I was lying along his side, my breasts brushing up against him. Eagerly, I slid down his zipper, guiding it past the large bulge in his shorts.

He wasn't wearing any underwear.

The only other time I ever looked at a man's privates was the one time I had sex—but that time had been in the dark, it had been very quick, and I certainly hadn't been presented with it the way I was now, and even though it was dark, the oversized moon shed just enough light for my hungry, curious eyes to explore.

He was larger than I expected. And it looked silky smooth, the skin pulled taut over a member that seemed to be reaching for me. Suddenly, I wanted all the fabric away. I didn't want his shorts anywhere near his body. and I tugged at them, making a frustrated sound.

He chuckled and reached beneath him, pulling something out and quickly dropping it beneath the hammock. I barely paid attention. My eyes never left his manhood. My hands begged to touch him.

Nash helped me pull off his shorts and he kicked them out of the hammock, where they landed in the sand.

Finally, he was completely bare. Finally, I could look at him the way I truly wanted.

"Just your heated gaze is enough to make me come," he murmured as he reached out and stroked my nipple.

But I wasn't only going to look.

Tentatively, I reached out to touch him with a single finger, trailing down to the base. He shuddered.

My eyes snapped up to his face, but he wasn't looking at me. His eyes were closed. Feeling a little bolder, I continued down, cupping his warm balls in my palm. The skin here felt a little different, a little less smooth, a little thinner, but it wasn't a bad feeling. I kneaded the round globes that rested just between his thighs, rolling them around gently in my hand while the other came up and wrapped around the base of his erection.

He groaned and I smiled. I moved my hand up and down along the length of him, enamored by the reactions I got whenever I touched him certain ways. His skin was utterly soft, almost like velvet, and I couldn't get enough of exploring him.

I encircled my thumb and forefinger around the tip, noting the way it got a little wider at the top, squeezing just a little. He jerked in my hand, his stomach muscles contracting at my touch. A small bead of moisture formed at the very top and I glanced up at him, a new desire forming in my mind.

His head was tilted back and I couldn't read his expression, so I scooted just a little closer, my face right in his pelvic area, my feet hanging off the hammock, and I wrapped my lips around his hardness. He tasted slightly salty and tangy. I licked at him like he was a giant lollipop and his hands grabbed the back of my head, his fingers digging into my scalp. His hips thrust forward, and I took him deep into my throat.

He groaned. As I moved my head back and forth, I cupped his balls again and massaged them gently.

[162]

Too soon, he reached down and pulled me away. I looked up, afraid I'd done something wrong, or maybe I'd been too overzealous and hurt him. "Nash," I whispered, my voice deep and husky. "Did I hurt you?"

"No, baby, you definitely didn't hurt me," he replied, carefully moving us so he was on top of me. I loved the feel of him over me, like I was small and protected, caged in by him.

His weight bore down as he brushed the hair away from my face. His lips grazed my cheek when he whispered, "Ava, I want to make love to you."

"I want that too," I whispered back.

Like he'd done it a hundred times before, he untied the strings on my bikini bottoms and tossed them away in the sand. He fitted himself between my legs, resting there. His long, hard length pressed against my core, resting right along my folds, the very tip of him sliding against my clitoris and making it hard for me to breathe.

Just when I thought my desire couldn't be any stronger, a new hunger swept through me.

He kissed me, a fiery kiss that scorched my skin, scorched my insides. It scorched my heart.

"I'll stop," he reminded me, pulling back just slightly. "You can change your mind."

"I know." I reached up and ran the backs of my fingers down his incredible face. His eyes deepened and fluttered closed. "I want this. I want you." He'd already made me feel so much that I wanted more; I wanted to see what else he could give me.

"I don't have any condoms. I didn't exactly prepare for this," he said, a hint of regret in his voice.

"I'm on the pill," I said as he kissed my nose, my cheek, and the corner of my lip.

He took my face in his hands and looked into my eyes. "I've never had sex without a condom before. I swear."

"I believe you."

He started kissing me again, deep, long kisses that had my hips searching for him as he moved against me but never slid inside.

Just when I thought I was going to go mad with need, he plunged in, one long, quick stroke. I opened my mouth, but no sound came out. I felt my body stretch out around him, hugging him tightly and welcoming him inside.

He cursed softly, burying his face in my neck and holding himself still. I wanted him to move. I rocked my hips, the movement sending shivers across his skin. He moaned in my ear and then rose up, pulling back and then plunging in again.

The hammock began to rock. The rope he used to tie it to the trees made a groaning sound as it rubbed against the trunk. He didn't seem to notice, but pulled out and plunged into me again. My body arched up as pleasure shot through me.

We proved to be too much for the hammock and it tipped, dumping us out. In the fall, Nash managed to wrap me in his arms and turn so he landed first and broke my fall.

I gasped and pushed off of him. "Are you okay?"

He groaned and grabbed my hips. I noticed then that I was straddling him, that he was still rock hard and he was pressing against me. I rocked against him, sliding along his pubic area. He moaned.

I rocked up, leaving some space between us, and his penis stood up, presenting the perfect opportunity for me to slide my body down over it.

Tiny waves of ecstasy rolled over me. The angle of him was different; the feel of him was stunning. I bucked my hips slowly, like I was sitting on a mechanical bull. My entire core was against him; every inch of me was in contact with him.

The friction of the short, rough curls on both our bodies drove me wild as we moved together. Little sounds erupted from my throat and chest. It was like I couldn't possibly get enough of him.

Oh, I definitely wasn't broken.

This was unbelievable.

This was more than I ever thought possible.

It was like my body was no longer my own. But it was ours. We moved as one. We breathed as one. We rose to the very pinnacle of pleasure as one.

I bent at the waist, bringing my chest up against his, and he wrapped his arms around me, anchoring me to him and then he started moving. Up until this point, I had set the pace; I had moved atop him with single-minded precision. But now he was taking control once more... He was holding me close and hammering into me, our hips banging together as pressure built inside me.

"Come with me, *bella*," he said and rocked upward, rubbing his pelvis against my super-sensitive clit while diving deep inside my body.

We both exploded. Everything fell away, everything but the ecstasy. Everything else around us was completely lost.

I don't know how long we floated, how long we lay there joined together. Eventually, he lifted me up like a ragdoll, and I hung limply above his body. He chuckled and kissed my forehead. He kissed each of my eyelids, and then he sighed. *"Mi adoro,"* he spoke in Spanish.

"What does that mean?" I asked, not bothering to lift my head off his chest.

"That I adore you."

I smiled.

17

I felt my heartbeat against my chest. It was a slow and steady rhythm, kind of lethargic and lazy. But that was because I was barely breathing. I was holding my breath.

He was touching me.

His fingers drifted over my skin like a breeze on a summer day. It was a feather-light caress that never ended because he didn't lift his hands.

It started at my collarbone and drifted out across my shoulders and then descended downward until he hooked his fingers around my elbow, brushing against the sensitive spot on the inside of my arm. Downward he traveled until his fingers pulled away from mine to hover just barely over the tops of my thighs.

Then his direction reversed, climbing upward so the slightly rough pads of his fingers traced the outline of my belly button and then dragged over my ribcage.

Tiny shivers raced up and down my spine, creating goose bumps that scattered over my scalp and caused my eyes to flutter closed.

His hands splayed my waist, gripping my flesh and pulling me closer, but he didn't kiss me. He buried his face inside my neck and used his tongue to wet a circle of tender skin, then pulled back slightly to blow across the area. I shuddered.

My body started to arch into him, but something caught my arm, something large and warm. It wrapped around my bicep in a possessive manner, causing my head to turn and cast a glance in the direction I was being pulled.

My heartbeat accelerated instantly. The lethargic rhythm was chased away by a shot of adrenaline so pure that I could taste it on my tongue.

He yanked me away from the teasing, gentle caresses and cupped my face in his palm, lowering his lips toward mine. Excitement crackled along my nerve endings and my tongue jutted out to moisten my lips.

Just as he was about to claim my kiss, I was yanked away again, this time by the one who had me first.

I cast a look to my left at green eyes flashing with possession and then once again to my right where chocolate eyes gleamed with jealousy.

I was caught in the middle of two very enticing choices.
A choice that I didn't want to make.

Brown eyes stepped closer, his body brushing against the entire length of my arm. He reached out and pushed the hair back over my shoulder, exposing the side of my face. He leaned down and captured my earlobe between his teeth and sucked it into his mouth. The gentle suckling sounds that whispered through my ear loosened something deep inside me.

I turned my head toward him, not wanting him to stop.
But green-eyes was not to be cast aside.

His palm covered my breast, gently kneading the area and causing my hardening nipple to brush against the smooth fabric of my bikini top. And then his mouth was on my neck, pulling the skin into his mouth and massaging it with his tongue.

Two mouths...

Two sets of hands...

And my single body.

I wasn't sure who to touch, who to grab, but I didn't want either of them to stop. The sensation of being kissed in more than one place in a single moment made a moan escape from my lips.

My fingers began to twitch, wanting to elicit shivers of their own.

As my hands lifted away from my sides, I vaguely wondered who they would reach for first...

My eyes shot open. I stared up at the dark summer sky and drew in a long, shaky breath.

Holy crap.

What the hell was that? A threesome... that's what that was. Never had I ever imagined myself and two guys getting it on at the same time. I might have been embarrassed if my body wasn't so incredibly turned on.

I squeezed my eyes shut as images taunted me, teased my mind and my body. Nash in front of me, Duke behind.

Neither wanted the other one there, but no one would walk away. The Ava man-wich had turned into the Ava buffet.

Thoroughly disturbed, I turned my head and looked at Nash, who was lying right beside me, looking peaceful in his sleep. How could I have a dream like that? How could I betray him that way?

And that's what it felt like. A betrayal.

I pushed up and walked quietly away, toward the water, where I stood, letting the surf rush over my feet and the wind tangle my hair. The moon was much higher now; the night seemed darker. But I didn't mind. I felt like hiding. Hiding from myself, that dream… my desires.

Maybe it was just stress. This wasn't exactly an easy situation. Added to the fact I practically lost my virginity (well, the actual first time clearly didn't count; I mean geesh, Nash made me feel more when he just looked at me) a few hours ago, well, maybe that dream wasn't as unsettling as I thought it should be.

A wave of homesickness swept over me, so strong that it hurt. I missed my family, my tiny apartment. I missed hunting for a new job, I missed worrying about paying the rent, and I even missed those annoying Friday night dinners when my family would ask me what I was going to do with my life.

Being here with everything essentially taken away made things seem clearer. It opened my eyes to facts I might not have wanted to see before. I was living my life in limbo—suspended between living and drifting. And it was all because I was scared.

What if I put myself out there like I did with my ex, like I did with my last job, only to have it blow up in my face again?

For so long I felt like a complete failure. A quitter. I quit school. I flitted between one job and the next. I finally gave up my virginity only be dumped and ridiculed. I finally committed to a job I liked, and I was let go because the economy sucked.

But I was still here.

I was still standing.

And now I was trapped on a deserted island with a guy I desperately wanted and a band of murdering pirates. To top it off, I was having dreams... dreams that were beginning to make sense.

Well, sort of.

What if those dreams were just one more way my mind was trying to get in the way of something I wanted? Trying to scare me away from getting too close to Nash?

"Ava?" His voice drifted through the breeze and squeezed my heart. I looked over my shoulder at Nash, who was standing there with sleep-heavy features and messy hair. He'd pulled on his shorts but hadn't bothered to button them or zip them up.

He came forward, wincing a little when his feet hit the cold water, but he didn't stop. He wrapped his arms around me from behind and rested his chin on my shoulder. "You still having bad dreams?"

"I didn't want to wake you," I said, avoiding the question. How did you tell a guy you had a sex dream about him... with another man?

"You can wake me anytime." He pressed a kiss to my bare shoulder. And then I realized...

"I'm still naked."

"I know" His voice turned husky.

"I miss home."

"I know. Me too."

"It's been almost a week. Do you think they've given up?"

"Would you have given up by now?" he asked.

I searched deep within myself for the answer. For the truth. "No. If it was someone I loved, I would never give up."

"They're going to find us, *bella.*"

"I like when you call me that."

"I know."

"You're a know-it-all."

I felt his chest vibrate with silent laughter. I brought up my hands to rest over his arms. I didn't want to let go of him. Not ever.

Conflicting thoughts swirled around my head. Finally, I sighed. Now wasn't the time to think too deeply about the way I felt about Nash.

Besides, my heart already made up its mind. It was just my head that was struggling. When I first met him, my body's response had been undeniable. But my head... my head reminded me that all guys were the same. Nash showed me differently. He proved me wrong. Yet my head was still fighting against what my heart already knew.

"What else is bothering you?" he whispered, reading me all too well. "Do you have regrets?"

I turned in his arms, tipping my head back and gazing up into his face. "I could never regret any of my time spent with you."

He kissed the tip of my nose. "That's good. I plan to take up a lot of your time." He swung me up into his arms, cradling me against his torso and walking out of the water and back up the beach where he spread me out in the sand and came over me.

For the rest of the night, I didn't think at all.

18

I woke up to a strange yet familiar sound. It wasn't the waves. It wasn't the ocean breeze. It wasn't gunshots or drums…

It was a plane.

Nash must have heard it too, and we both bolted up off the sand and rushed out by the water, staring at the sky and waving our arms frantically, trying to get the pilot's attention.

But the plane was nowhere in sight.

Yet we could both hear it. It had to be nearby.

But where?

"We need a flare," Nash said, frenzied. "We need the flare gun on the plane!"

We both took off running down the beach. He ran so fast he went out of sight as I struggled to push through the sand, thoroughly disgusted with myself.

I kept glancing up at the sky, trying to catch just a glimpse of the aircraft, praying that it wouldn't turn and fly off, leaving us stranded once more.

When I finally reached the part of the beach where I could see our crashed plane, I rushed forward, wondering what on earth was taking Nash so long. As fast as he moved, I really expected to see the bright-red burn of a flare across the sky by now.

Seconds dragged by.

He never reappeared.

The sound of the overhead aircraft faded away.

Finally, Nash came running out of the trees, the big flare gun clasped in his hand. He had this wild look on his face. The minute his feet touched the sand, he looked up into the sky.

"Fuck!" he screamed, frustrated. "Did you see the plane?" he asked.

I shook my head no.

"Grab up whatever you can find—wood, shells, whatever. We're going to write out S.O.S. in the sand."

I ran off to grab some of the partially burned wood left in the bonfire and some large palm fronds and driftwood lying around. As I started to build the first S, Nash came over beside me and yanked something out of his back pocket.

"What is that?" I asked as I worked.

"Make it big," he instructed, looking at my handiwork. Then he explained. "This is a smoke flare."

It was a long, red stick (probably would be better to call it a wand, but whatever), and I watched as he ripped the top off and jammed it in his pocket. Then he pulled the cap off the top and stuck it on his finger like an oversized thimble. He held the flare out and scrapped his covered finger over it once and it burst forward like the giant sparklers I used to play with on the Fourth of July.

"Don't look into the flame," he told me, and I looked away, starting to make the O.

When I ran out of supplies, I stood to get more, and I noticed the bright flames had gone out and there was now a deep rust-colored smoke funneling up into the sky, being caught up in the wind.

"It's too windy!" I worried.

He shook his head. "Smoke flares are designed to be seen from miles away and in the windiest conditions. Maybe it will attract that plane back."

It was certainly better than nothing. I rushed forward to get some more supplies, but he grabbed my arm. "Stay away from the plane."

The look in his eyes worried me, but I could only deal with one thing at a time so I nodded and then rushed around for more rocks and fallen branches. When I came back, Nash buried the end of the smoke flare in the sand (in the center of the letter O), keeping it upright as smoke poured into the sky.

"That's going to attract *their* attention," I said, implying the pirates.

"They already know we're here," he said grimly.

He didn't say anything else as we finished the S.O.S signal, and my mind raced wildly, wondering what he meant. At the same time, I listened to the plane, praying it would turn back.

Please see the smoke.

The signal was done and the smoke was still gliding up above the ocean when Nash grabbed my hand and pulled me along with him toward the hammock.

"What's going on?" I asked, trying to hold in my freak-out and wondering how long it would last.

"They know we're here."

"The pirates?" I whispered.

He nodded.

"How?"

"I don't know, but they were in the plane. They searched it. They trashed it."

If my body wasn't producing adrenaline before, it definitely was now. "They must have seen us yesterday."

"Yeah. It was damn good luck we spent the night in that hammock or we would have been there." He actually shuddered, like the thought of that was absolutely repulsive.

"How many do you think there are?"

"Way more than us."

"What are we going to do?"

"Stay out of sight," he said as we walked up to the hammock. "Stay on the move. Pray that someone sees that smoke."

When we reached the hammock swaying gently in the breeze, he turned his back to me, reaching beneath the sand, and picked something up. A memory of him pulling something out of his pants last night and putting it there drifted through my head.

I wasn't curious what it was then.

I sure as hell was now.

"What's that?" I asked.

He turned and showed me.

It was a gun. A black pistol.

My mouth went dry. My voice was hoarse when I spoke. "What happens if they find us, Nash?"

Tempt

"We hope to God I have enough bullets."

19

I was beginning to think the universe had it out for us. I mean, really. First we nosedive from the sky, land on a deserted island, get stranded, and now there was an angry hoard of murdering pirates sulking around this island, searching for us.

This was officially the worst vacation ever.

Only it wasn't a vacation... It had started out as a tribute to my grandmother.

I gasped and stopped walking, digging my feet into the sand. Nash swung around, his wide eyes searching everything in the immediate space around me. "What is it?"

"Kiki!"

His mouth flattened in a grim line.

"I'm going back for her."

"No."

"Yes, I am."

"Your grandmother would not want you to risk your life for her."

"What would you do?" I asked quietly, leaning into him. "If that was your grandmother? If it was someone you loved?"

I saw the defeat in his eyes almost instantly. "Don't even try to stop me from doing what you would absolutely do."

I marched away, back toward the plane and the smoke-filled sky.

"Ava," he said, rushing to my side and pulling me close. "Stay at my side."

"Do you think I'm so defenseless?" I asked, irritated. I mean, yeah, I wasn't going to be running any marathons (okay, fine, not even around the block) anytime soon, but I was far from helpless.

"Of course not."

"Look, I love that you're so protective. I actually really love it, even though it annoys the crap out of me sometimes, but you can't protect me from everything."

"I know. But this, *this* I have to protect you from."

"What *this*?" I asked, trying to see through the smoke toward the plane.

"What do you think a group of known thieves and killers—a group of *men*—who live on an island with no law would do to a blond-haired, blue-eyed beauty like you?"

A vision of those chains and the dark crimson stain on the rocks flashed before me. A vision of being locked in that tiny, gross shack assaulted me.

I can't even describe how terrified his words made me.

"I'm not trying to control you, *bella*," Nash said gently, stroking a hand down my arm. "There's only one of me and many of them. I will fight to the death for you, but when I die, so does your protection."

A sob caught in my throat.

I was so overwhelmed with emotion, I stopped walking. Thick smoke wrapped around us, likely concealing us and this little stretch of beach where we stood. He said he would die for me. The thought of him dying literally made me feel like I had ice in my veins.

I threw my arms around him and buried my face in his neck. "Please don't die."

"Ahh, *bella*, I don't have plans on doing that anytime soon."

I pulled back just inches so I could stare into his beautiful face. A face that songs were written about. "I would rather take whatever those pirates did to me than let you die trying to keep me safe. I would not trade my life for yours. Never."

He kissed me. It was a hard kiss, the kind tinged with desperation and smoke. His arms tightened so much that I thought my ribs might crack, but I didn't say anything because I was holding him just as hard.

He tore his mouth away and heaved a breath. "We have to go. They're going to come back when they see that smoke. If we want to get Kiki, we have to move."

I nodded.

He took my hand and together we ran the rest of the distance to the plane. This time I kept up. It was easier to run faster when you were running for your life. And for the life of someone else.

We rushed along the side of the plane, ducking low (who knows why) and creeping around to the back end. Nash kept his body in front of mine at all times and peered into the plane before escorting me inside.

What once was a makeshift "cozy" home was now a complete disaster. The poor plane had not only seen a crash, but now a crowd of vile criminals and was down for the count. All the windows were bashed out, including what was left of the windshield. All the controls in the cockpit were smashed and destroyed. My suitcase was overturned. Shampoo was poured on the floor; my clothes were ripped and scattered about. All the fruit was squished; the newly smashed food drew flies like a pile of manure. The chairs were slashed, and all the water was dumped out.

I blinked, trying not to focus on the mess, but concentrate on the reason we were here. Kiki. My grandmother's ashes were the most important thing I had here. I couldn't lose them.

We searched.

We searched everywhere.

I started to cry. Big, fat silent tears that I couldn't stop but didn't want Nash to see.

I was still searching frantically, still pawing through the mess, when I felt his hand rest on my shoulder. I knew what that hand meant. I knew exactly.

"No," I groaned. *"No."*

"It's not here, *bella*," he said gently.

"Who would do that? Who would steal what was left of someone's body?" I cried.

"Monsters," he said, pulling me up and hooking an arm around my waist. "We gotta go. We've been here too long."

There wasn't anything else I could do but let him lead me away. I knew I would never see this plane again. Maybe because we would make it home. Maybe because we wouldn't. I really didn't know.

But I did know the chances of us dying here were bigger than the chances of us leaving.

We hopped out of the plane, and he wrapped his arm around me again. "Let's stay in the trees. They offer more coverage."

We walked to where the mangos grew. Nash loaded some in his cargo pockets and I carried a few in my hands. I wished I wasn't wearing this stupid dress. I needed pockets. Instead, I held up the hem like a basket and dropped in the fruit.

I could have sworn I caught Nash looking at my legs. But surely he wasn't looking at something like that at a time like this.

Well, okay, he *was* a guy.

Once we gathered all we could carry, he glanced up toward the sky. "We need to find some sort of shelter or a place to hide. It's going to get dark and they will have an advantage."

"How?"

"Because they know this island. A lot better than we do. They'll probably still search, even in the night."

"Where will we go?" I frowned, searching my mind for a place we might have seen where we could hide.

"I have an idea," he said, taking my hand and leading me back the way we came. We circled around a few times. We passed the same flowers several times. I knew we weren't lost. He was making sure we weren't being followed, that no one was watching.

Finally, we came close to the lagoon. Nash picked up a couple rocks and threw them one at a time into the water, each one of them making a distinct plopping sound.

After that, we stood, for what felt like days, and waited. We waited and we watched, nerves stirring inside me that someone was there, that the noise he made would draw out some dirty scoundrel with dreadlocks.

No one came. There were no sounds but the birds and wildlife. None of it ever paused or drew quiet. I took that as a positive sign. Surely, the wildlife would cease to make noise if danger were around.

Right?

Or was that just in movies?

When I got home, I was not only taking up running, but I was going to learn about survival—aka: how not to die.

"C'mon," he said, leading us out of the protection of the foliage and over to the water. He pressed his finger to his lips and then slipped into the water quietly. He motioned for me to follow so I did, holding close the little bunch of mangos.

We moved slowly. It was hard to tread with only one arm, but I did it because losing our only food was not an option. The entire time we swam, I kept a constant watch on the edges of the water. Every sound, every echo in the air caused my heart to pound and my body to tighten.

If someone showed up now... we would be sitting ducks.

Nash did the same thing, swimming quietly with one arm, holding the pistol and the flare gun up out of the water.

Finally, we reached the waterfall and he went around to the very edge and slipped around it, hunching over the guns to keep them as dry as he could. I waited cautiously on the other side until I heard his whisper that all was safe.

I swam to the rock where Nash was already sitting. He reached into the water and yanked me up, draping my exhausted body over the slippery wet surface.

I dumped the fruit toward the back and stifled a cough, leaning up against the back of the little cove. Nash squeezed in beside me, placing the guns as far from the water as he could.

"Did they get wet?"

"Only a little. I think they'll still work."

"This is a good place to hide."

"It keeps our backs safe. Now we only have to watch one direction, and the water makes a good shield and it will muffle any sounds we make."

"Now what?" I asked him.

He handed me a mango. "We eat. We sleep and we wait for morning."

"And then?"

"And then we hope the plane comes back. If it doesn't, we're going to have to figure out something else."

"Like what?"

"Maybe we can make one of those boats work."

"Maybe we could sneak onto the pirates' boat and take that one."

"Maybe," he echoed.

We ate in silence. My body was starved, but I wasn't hungry at all. Night fell, and inside the little cove seemed darker than any place I'd ever been.

There was no light here at all because the moon and the stars had no way of getting in. I could barely see two feet in front of me except for the movement of the water, which sometimes looked a little silver in the dark.

With the darkness came the cold.

We were inside a dark, damp place that the sun never touched, so it never held any heat. The cold seemed to seep into my skin and go straight for my bones.

I tucked my hands between my thighs, squeezing them tightly together, and tried to keep them from shaking.

Nash reached for me in the dark, pulling me between his legs, pulling his in, tucking them around me. Then he wrapped his arms around my chest, literally wrapping himself around my body. He was warmer and the warmth made me moan a little.

He rested his chin on my shoulder and we sat there together just breathing.

My eyes began to grow heavy and every now and then, I would catch myself nodding off to sleep and I would jerk awake, trying not to give in to my body's needs.

"Go to sleep, *bella*," he murmured. "I'll keep watch for a while."

"You can't stay awake all night."

"Once I'm sure it's safe, I'll go to sleep too."

"Don't let go," I whispered.

His grip tightened.

20

It was still dark when I woke up. I wasn't sure what caused me to wake, but judging from the fact that my butt was completely asleep and felt like it was being stabbed by a thousand tiny needles, I figured it was because I sat too long in the same position. I was still sitting with Nash, but he was sprawled backward, leaning up against the rock, and one of his legs was under mine and we were sort of tangled up in each other.

But not in a sexual way.

In a *your body will make you pay for this later* way.

I slowly eased away from Nash and stood, stretching out my arms and back and trying not to grit my teeth against the sting in my rump.

My clothes were still damp and it wasn't too comfortable, and my hair felt like a tangled mess. A day at the spa sounded like heaven right then.

Maybe if I closed my eyes and pretended I was there…

"Ava? Are you back there?"

My eyes popped open. Was someone talking? I glanced around at Nash. He was still sleeping. His position was horrible. His butt was going to be sore tomorrow.

"Ava?"

"Duke?" I whispered. I looked through the waterfall, but all I could see was darkness. I was afraid to call out, afraid that it wasn't actually him.

What if my ears were playing tricks on me? What if it was the pirates? What if they were trying to lure me into giving away our position?

I stood there and listened for a long time. I thought about waking up Nash, but I couldn't do it. He had to be exhausted. I knew he was worried about being here... about me being vulnerable. He needed the sleep. So did I.

Who knew what tomorrow would bring?

I moved back over to sit down once more when I heard another sound. It sounded like a low moan or a cry of pain. I moved to the side, trying to see around the water. I caught a little bit of movement near the shore.

I grabbed the gun off the ground and held it up to my chest, knowing I would use it if I had too but knowing I would be a terrible shot. It would be a waste of good bullets.

I sucked in a deep, nervous breath. "Duke?"

"Yes, it's me."

"What are you doing?"

"I'm hurt... I need a place to hide. I need help."

Concern for his well-being had me stepping forward, but I stopped. "How'd you get hurt?"

"They found me..." His voice trailed away. "I got away..."

He fell silent. I waited for him to speak again. He didn't.

"Duke?"

"Can I come over there?" he asked, his voice low and strained.

"Of course." I certainly wouldn't deny him help. After all, he had helped us.

I heard a light splash and the sound of him moving through the water. He swam close enough that I could make out the shape of him just on the other side of the fall. When I thought he would come through, he didn't.

He stopped moving.

He seemed to bob in the water, sinking low and then reappearing.

"Duke?"

"Tired," he said and went under again.

How injured was he? Was he so hurt that he was going to drown tying to get to safety? I slipped into the water, swimming toward the falls where I could just make out his shape.

"Grab my hand," I told him, reaching through the chilly curtain of water, extending my fingers to him.

"Thank you," he murmured, and I felt him grasp me. I went to pull him in, but he was too heavy. His hand started to slip away.

He grasped me at the last second and I breathed a sigh of relief. He tugged, trying to get a better grip. More of my body slipped beneath the water.

"Swim closer," I told him, struggling to keep afloat.

All of a sudden, his hold on me turned forceful. The bones in my fingers screamed for relief. I opened my mouth to call out, to tell him he was hurting me, but I was yanked through the water, rewarded with a mouth and nose full.

I tried to pull away.

He wouldn't let go.

He yanked me right up against him... and then he shoved me under.

Water enveloped me like a thick, dark blanket. It pulled me in the wrong direction, and I tried to push up... but he was holding me down.

He was trying to drown me.

I wasn't going to drown.

I hadn't survived everything just to let someone kill me in a split second just feet from Nash. If I died while he was sleeping, he would never forgive himself.

I started to fight. To thrash around in the water.

My knee connected with something soft and he tensed, his grip loosening. I slid away, my head breaking free of the surface. I gasped for much needed air and then called for Nash.

He yanked me back under again.

He placed his hands on my shoulders and shoved me under. I felt bubbles release from my mouth and nose. My lungs began to burn. It was beyond painful. I wanted to breathe. My body had the intense urge to suck in... but that would only fill my lungs with water.

Something heavy plunged into the water behind me and a swell of waves rocked my body, pulling me from under Duke. But he grabbed me back, his fingers digging into my shoulders.

My thinking started to grow dim, my brain fuzzy. There was a commotion in the water... probably one of those man-eating piranha's come to make me its dinner.

The heavy weight of the water was suddenly lifted. Oxygen teased my nose and I began to cough. Something was towing me through the water with purpose, with a strong grip.

He lifted me up onto the rock, flinging back my body, and my limbs worked to scramble up, but they were weak. He cursed, a naughty four-letter word, and then I slid back in the water for a few long seconds while he sprang out and then towed me up.

"Ava," Nash said urgently. His hands tapped my face. "Wake up."

I coughed again, a little water trickling out of my mouth, and he sat me up, supporting my body with his weight.

"What happened?"

"He said he was hurt," I whispered. "I was trying to help him."

Nash swore again. "We can't stay here now. He knows where we are. We're sitting ducks."

"I'm sorry," I said pitifully.

"Don't be sorry. This isn't your fault." Underneath his soothing tone was a voice of steel. He was angry. Thankfully his anger was directed at Duke and not me.

I coughed again, trying hard to muffle the sound. I was so confused. Part of me wondered if maybe Duke's behavior was an accident. If maybe he was so injured he fell into the water and pulled me with him, unable to help either of us.

But I'd felt his hands on my shoulders.

I felt him holding me under.

Why would he do that? I thought we were friends.

I began to shake, cold seeping into my wet body. Nash pulled me closer, wrapping his arms around me.

"Daylight can't be long now. Feels like we've been in this cave forever," he murmured, rubbing warmth up and down my arms. "I think we should wait it out 'til light. Us leaving now would only put them at an advantage. It's dark. I don't know if he was alone. Daylight will allow us to at least see what we're dealing with."

"Why would he do that?" I asked pathetically.

"I don't know, *bella.* I don't know."

And so we sat there—wet, cold, and alert— wondering what the hell awaited us when the sun finally rose.

21

Gray-ish first light of day began to seep through the screen of water, chasing away the deepest of the darkness and bringing some semblance of comfort. I knew we were still in grave danger. I knew there were things going on here that we knew nothing about. Yet there was a sort of security in the daylight—even the palest of day—that made things seem just tiny bit more manageable.

My body was stiff. My joints ached from sitting cold and tense the entire night. Nash had barely moved, keeping himself tucked around me like some professional bodyguard hell-bent on keeping his charge alive. And I knew that if it wasn't for him, I would already be dead.

I would have been dead three times over by now.

I owed him my life.

I wanted to give him my heart.

"I think this was the longest night of my entire life," he said gruffly, right next to my ear.

"It must still be early," I whispered.

"I haven't heard any movement outside. Have you?"

"No."

He moved, sitting back a little, reaching behind us, and then a mango appeared under my nose. "Breakfast is served."

"I don't think I can eat."

"Take it," he said, pushing it toward me. "Don't know when the next meal will be."

I took it and ate. He was right. A distant rumble had me looking up, toward the sky I couldn't see. "Was that thunder?"

He snorted. "It would rain right now."

"Maybe we should stay here."

"We need to move. I don't know what Duke is planning. He could lead the pirates right to us."

"Why would he do that?"

"That's the million-dollar question."

"Where will we go?"

"I've been thinking about that," he said, picking up another mango and sinking his teeth into the flesh. "I think we should move toward the other side of the island."

"You want to go *closer* to the enemy?"

He paused in chewing and looked at me, his eyes warming a little. "Look at you talking like we're in a spy movie."

"This only happens to people in the movies."

He grinned. For a moment, things felt normal. They felt relaxed. Then reality came back. Rain broke through the sky with another clap of thunder, and heavy, insistent drops began pounding the water beyond the falls.

They hit against the rocks overhead and plopped in the lagoon, setting the water to waving.

The sound of the rain was so heavy that it almost drowned out the waterfall, and the thunder continued to roll. Maybe it was later than we thought; maybe the sky was just gray with the storm.

"Anyway," Nash said, ignoring the storm and throwing the pit of the mango into the water. "They won't be expecting us to come closer. They will expect us to try and get away."

I nodded slowly, seeing the logic behind his words.

"They will likely be scouring the island for us. Maybe there won't be many of them left at their camp. I think if we want an opportunity to take their boat—or one of the other ones, now is the time to do it."

He was right, of course. The longer we waited, the weaker we became. Eventually those pirates were going to completely drive us away from this water source. We would grow weak from dehydration... We would grow tired from running, exhausted from lack of sleep. If we were going to escape, now was the time to do it.

"Let's do it," I said.

"We're going to be very vulnerable in the water, trying to get to shore. Can you swim underwater, hold your breath?"

I nodded.

"I'm going to go first. I'll wait on the shore for you. Swim as far as you can beneath the water, out of sight. When you reach the shore, I'll pull you up. Be ready to run. We'll go for cover and then stop to make sure we aren't being followed."

"What about you?"

"I'm going to do the same." I watched him tuck the flare gun into a cargo pocket on his shorts.

"Can that get wet?"

"I hope the hell so. It should still work."

"What about the pistol?"

He looked grim. "That can't get wet. I'll try to keep it dry."

"Be careful," I whispered as he lowered himself in the water and reached for the pistol, holding it high over his head.

We didn't say anything else as he eased around the edge of the waterfall, trying to shield the gun from the worst of the water. I slid into the water and swam to just behind the falling drops, fastening my eyes on Nash. He swam out a little ways and then he chucked the gun.

He literally threw it onto the shore.

I listened for the sound of it blasting. I cringed at the thought of it giving us away. But it landed with a silent thud and didn't go off.

Nash slipped below the surface of the water and completely disappeared from sight. The rain made it impossible to see any ripples he might have made as he swam. It seemed like forever when I saw his head resurface as he pushed up on shore.

I wasted no time, taking a deep breath and going under the water. I tried really hard not to be creeped out by the dark, cold water. I kept my eyes tightly shut, not wanting to see if there was anything swimming around in here with me.

Just when I started to feel like I needed air, something reached into the water and pulled me up.

My first thought was to fight, but I recognized that touch. I trusted it.

Nash hauled me out of the water and we took off, into the coverage of trees, and ducked behind giant palm fronds dripping with rainwater.

"I can't believe that worked," Nash said, a rueful smile playing on his lips.

"You mean you thought we would get caught?"

He shrugged his shoulders sheepishly.

I rolled my eyes. *Men.*

"Last time, we went sort of around the island, in an arc. This time let's cut straight across," he said, keeping his voice low.

We waited for what felt like forever as we watched the surrounding area for signs of pirates. For signs of Duke. "Where do you think he went?" I whispered.

"I hope the bastard drowned."

I glanced at him.

"I hit him hard enough. I hope he blacked out and sank to the bottom of that lagoon. He'll feed the fish for weeks."

I shuddered. I was almost fish food.

Nash swore lightly and pulled me into his side. "Sorry. That was harsh."

"It's okay."

"I don't think I've ever been so pissed. Waking up and seeing that douche bag trying to drown you. I swear if he shows his face, I'm going to shoot his ass."

"I haven't seen anyone, have you?"

"No." He took my hand. "Let's go."

We moved through the island with a little more speed than a casual stroll. The heavy rain made the ground slippery, but I managed to stay sort of dry. The large leaves overhead acted like a makeshift umbrella, keeping the worst of the water at bay. If we weren't on the run from people with nefarious and still unknown plans, the sound of the raindrops hitting the leaves would be lovely. It was the kind of sound, the kind of day, that normally would make me want to curl up with a book and a blanket.

But there would be no reading today.

Just running for our lives.

We walked for several hours, stopping every so often to duck into dense foliage, to drink a little bit of rainwater that gathered around the plants.

I began to wonder how much longer we had when voices carried through the rain. Nash tensed and pulled me into a bush where we had to lie on our bellies to be properly hidden.

"You find them yet?" someone yelled.

"No."

"Can't believe he let her get away."

"He'll pay for it."

Were they talking about Duke? What did he have to do with any of this? I really hadn't wanted to believe that he was involved at all. He had been so nice... so lonely... cute even. Was all that just an act?

I sucked in a breath when a pair of bare feet came close. So close that I could have reached out and touched them.

I couldn't help but notice that he desperately needed a pedicure. I mean, really, just because he's some thief and killer didn't mean he couldn't worry about good hygiene.

Right in front of us the feet stopped, turned in our direction.

Everything fell silent.

The world stopped turning.

My heart stopped beating.

Then gnarly-toed pirate grunted. He turned and walked away. "They ain't over here. They'd be stupid to come to our side."

"She don't have to be smart to give me what I'm after," replied a voice from farther away.

The men laughed.

I gagged.

Nash put his hand over my mouth and gave me a stern look.

Eventually, their footsteps died away. Their voices grew too faint to hear. All that was left was the continuous sound of the rain and Nash's and my erratic breathing.

"That was way too fucking close," he breathed out.

"Did you see his toenails?" I shuddered. "Gross."

"They practically called you their new plaything and you're worried about his toes?" He gaped at me.

I shrugged. I would rather worry about the fungus growing beneath his raggedy nails (trust me, there *had* to be fungus) than think about being raped and tortured.

"Come on," he said, belly crawling out from under the bush and reaching in to help me.

When he started to walk, I pulled him back. "I don't think I've told you thank you."

His eyes met mine.

"For everything you've done for me. For being strong, for never acting like we wouldn't make it

[198]

home. For keeping me warm, for protecting me, for being you."

He brushed the side of my face with his knuckles. "You didn't thank me for the best sex of your life."

I giggled. "Thanks for that too."

Gently, he drew me closer, bringing my body right up against his. I loved the feel of his skin beneath my cheek. I hugged him tight, trying to tell him everything that no words could ever express.

"I can't imagine being stranded with anyone but you," he whispered.

A few minutes later, he pulled away. I wanted to pull him back, but I knew I couldn't. "Come on," he said quietly. "We need to keep moving."

We trudged on, the sound of the beach drawing closer. I breathed a sigh of relief. The other side of the island was near. For the first time all night and all day, I felt hope... Surely there was some sort of boat we could make work.

Hell, at this point, I'd sail away in one with a hole in it. I'd take my chances at sinking before I took my chances with the people on this island.

The foliage began to thin slightly and through it, I caught the sight of the distant sand and beach. I was just about to thank God for helping us get this far when something happened.

Something that stole away all my hope.

Nash, who was a few yards ahead of me, stepped unknowingly on some sort of booby trap. The minute his foot hit the ground, a net came up off the ground, palms and leaves raining off of it. It swung him up high, dangling from a tree, swaying just above me, sorely out of reach.

"Nash!" I whisper-yelled.

Our eyes connected. His mouth was set in a hard line. His green eyes were grim.

"Run."

"What?" I said, not really comprehending.

"You need to run."

"I can't leave you!" I started searching around for a way to free him, desperately looking for something sharp.

"Ava!" he snapped. "Get the hell out of here. Hide."

I stopped and looked up. I felt my lower lip wobble. I couldn't leave him.

Behind us, men were crashing through the woods, yelling and whooping about their catch.

Fear unparalleled to anything else trampled me.

Nash pulled the flare gun out of his shorts and worked it through the net, dropping it from the sky and into my hands. "Get to the beach, shoot this straight up into the sky. Hide. And don't you come out until you hear a plane."

"But…"

"Do it," he growled.

I hesitated again.

"I'll find you, Ava. I promise."

The men were much closer now. My heart started to pound. I looked over my shoulder and caught the first sight of them. I took off running, tearing through the woods and ripping out into the sand.

One of the men yelled. I heard someone cheer. My steps faltered. How could I just leave him there? Literally dangling in the sky with no defense.

He has a gun. Get help.

The thought spurred me on. I took off running again, ignoring how hard it was to push through the sand. I had to get help. I couldn't let him die.

I ended up near the center of the pirate's camp. I stopped. I lifted the gun straight up to the sky, pointing the muzzle toward the dark, churning storm clouds.

I pulled the trigger.

The flare shot out with alarming speed. My arm recoiled a bit and I dropped the gun, watching as a trail of red blasted through the open sky. It lit up the dark clouds, everything glowing a bright burning red.

Please, God, let someone see.

Part of me was very afraid the storm would keep the rescuers away. Part of me whispered that this was it. We were going to die.

I wouldn't accept that.

And I wasn't going to hide.

I ran toward the boat graveyard, hell-bent on finding some sort of weapon. But my need for a weapon was momentarily derailed when I saw my suitcase. The one with Kiki in it. A small cry of relief ripped from my throat and I changed course, running to it, refusing to leave her behind.

I was so focused on getting to the object of my desire and getting something to help Nash that I didn't hear him approach.

He pounced on me from behind, tackling me in the sand, his weight pinning me down.

I started to scream.

22

"Shut up," he said as he flipped me over and pressed his hand over my mouth.

I froze and stared up at Duke. He was pale. His long hair was wild and he was soaking wet.

I bit his hand.

He howled and released my mouth. I brought my fist down and connected with his fragile man parts. He rolled off me and I scrambled to my feet and took off.

He caught me in seconds, spinning me back around.

"Why are you doing this?" I spat, looking around for a weapon. There was nothing here. I needed to get to the boats.

"Do you think I want to do this?" he asked. "I don't. But I don't have a choice."

"I'm pretty sure you have a choice."

"You're right. I do… It's life or death. Your death for my life."

I swallowed. Well, I didn't care for those odds.

My eyes wandered back to the woods and I thought about Nash.

"He's a dead man," Duke growled.

In hindsight, I realized that leaping at him to cause bodily harm was not the best idea I ever had. But even knowing how it was going to end, I still would have done it again. Anger bubbled up inside me and I clawed at his face and neck, desperate to inflict any kind of pain that I could.

He backhanded me.

I fell.

He dragged me across the sand, toward the rocks...

Toward the chains.

I started to fight. To kick and yell.

"Keep fighting, honey," he drawled. "Those assholes love a challenge."

I went limp. Revulsion rippled through me.

He slammed me up against the rocks and proceeded to clamp one of the chain cuffs around my wrist.

I struggled and kicked, swinging my free fist around and connecting with his cheek.

He stopped and looked at me. "I guess I deserved that."

"Why are you doing this, Duke? I liked you."

Regret shined in his eyes. Some of the determined craziness seeped away. He pushed his hands through his tangled hair, tucking it behind his ears.

"Do you know what it's like?" he murmured. "To be trapped here, day after day, week after week. Alone. Knowing that no one will come for you?"

"I think I might have an idea."

[203]

"You have no idea," he growled.

"Then tell me," I implored, tucking my free hand behind my back between the rock and me. I prayed he would forget one arm was still loose.

"They attacked my boat. They came out of nowhere, speeding right up alongside me. At first I thought they were just sailors passing through. It became apparent they weren't the closer they drew. My little boat was no match for their bigger engine," he said, lost in memory, his eyes looking far away. "I don't know why they would waste their time on such a small boat. Why they would bother with a guy like me. I barely had any money. I didn't want any trouble. I gave them everything and told them I would jump overboard. That I would likely drown on the way home. I wish I had drowned."

"What happened to you, Duke?" I whispered, gazing at the scar in his eyebrow, remembering the scar I saw on his back.

"They kidnapped me. They forced me here to this island. I became their whipping boy. Their servant, their pet."

He yanked off his shirt and threw it into the sand.

He turned, showing me the many crisscrossing scars that covered his back. Some were newer than others; some were raised and puckered.

Emotion clogged my throat. I knew then that these chains, the bloodstains on this rock, were likely his. I suddenly felt terribly sorry for him. "Oh, Duke."

"They forced me to rob boats for them." He continued, still showing me his back. I wanted to shut my eyes to the horrible sight, but I didn't. "I don't look like a criminal. I don't look like a dirty pirate.

They would use me to get close to boaters. I would pretend to need help and the owners would invite me onto their ship. And the pirates would converge. They would take over the boat. They would kill men and rape women."

"All for money." I choked.

"And then they would beat me. They would taunt me and say I would never go home."

"But why would you do this to me? You know Nash and I... we wanted to help you. We meant it when we said we would take you home."

He laughed. A hollow sound. "You're not getting off this island. There is no getting away."

"We will." I insisted.

"They knew you were here the minute that plane crashed," he went on. "They came to investigate immediately. Nothing happens on this island that they don't know about. At first they thought you were dead. They saw your bodies and figured you hadn't survived. It was only later when I saw you that I knew you'd survived."

"You were nice to us. You showed us food."

"You catch more bees with honey."

"You pretended to like me..." I trailed away, my head spinning, trying to make sense of what he was saying. I felt stupid. Utterly idiotic for falling for his longing looks, his smiles, his teasing. He was trying to tempt me away from Nash this entire time.

Only I would never be tempted away from someone like him.

"I realized fast that wasn't going to work. He was getting in the way."

"Did you set that trap?" I glanced back at the forest. Things were too quiet.

"I had to get him out of the way. They only want you. They don't want him."

My anxiety spiked and I tried to get away. I strained against the chain that held me. I had to get to Nash. I couldn't let him die. I didn't care what happened to me anymore so long as he was safe.

The distant sound of a plane shocked me back from panic. "Help!" I screamed. "Help us!"

I knew they couldn't hear me. I knew they couldn't see me. But I couldn't stop screaming. I screamed and screamed.

Duke just stared at me like I was stupid for trying.

"Do you hear that?" I said. "It's a plane. They saw the flare. We can escape. You can come with us."

I could see his mind churning. "You would let me come?"

"Yes!" I lied. "This is our chance to be free! Please, unchain me!"

He pulled the key from his pocket and pondered it in his palm.

A gunshot cut through the wind and the dwindling rain.

I started to sob. I yelled Nash's name over and over until my voice was hoarse. Oh my God, if he was dead I might as well die too.

And then a plane flew overhead.

I started jumping, waving my arm, screaming anew. "Help us! Get their attention!" I cried at Duke. "Please!"

He shot into action, running below the plane and waving his arms, jumping up and down. It drew closer and I realized it wasn't a plane, but a helicopter. It was red.

The Coast Guard.

Dear God, the Coast Guard had found us.

Movement at the edge of the sand drew my attention. Nash burst forward, running like the wind. His chest was splattered with red and I screamed his name.

His head snapped to me and he changed course, rushing toward the rocks as several scurvy pirates followed.

"Help!" I screamed again into the sky.

The helicopter was lowering, the wind battering the little aircraft, and yet it still came closer. "Please don't leave," I pleaded.

Duke ran back over, making a beeline for me. But Nash intercepted him, tackling him to the ground and hitting him in the head with the butt of the gun. He sprawled out beneath him and Nash pushed up, rushing over to me.

"He has the key!" I cried, pointing at Duke.

Nash cursed and rushed away. Pirates were closing in as Nash dug through Duke's pocket and came up with the single key.

Just before he reached me, the pirates caught up to him. He threw the key at me. It landed in the sand at my feet. My hands were shaking so badly that I had a hard time getting the key in the tiny hole.

I gave a frustrated cry and the key slid in.

The gun went off again.

I fell forward when the chain released me. I scrambled up and ran toward Nash, who was wielding the gun as a bleeding pirate lay at his feet. The others were circling him warily as I rushed to his side.

He put his arm around me, draping me in security, as the helicopter hovered above.

[207]

"We cannot land," echoed a loud voice from overhead. "Put down your weapons."

Surely they could see that people were trying to kill us! "Help!" I screamed.

A very long, very unsteady ladder fell from the helicopter and landed in the sand. "Drop your weapons," they instructed again.

Nash looked between the gun and the pirates. Between us and the rope ladder offering us safety.

"Get ready to run," he said to me.

I nodded.

He dropped the gun.

We took off.

Nash took my hand and dragged me behind him, my feet barely touching the sand. Just when the ladder was within reach, a hand closed around my ankle.

I shrieked and fell, rolling over and looking behind me.

One of the dirty pirates had launched at me, managing to take me down. I kicked at him with my free leg. That only seemed to make him try harder.

Nash grabbed me beneath the armpits and pulled, trying to get me away. A strange game of tug-of-war ensued... I was the rope. I was the prize.

Safety or death? Live or Die?

I glanced at Nash. "Just let me go. Save yourself."

He yelled a cuss word. A very bad one.

And then a gunshot cut through the commotion. The man tugging my leg fell into the sand as a pool of red spread out beneath him. Nash pulled me away, lifting me up and carrying me the rest of the way to the ladder. He stepped on and wrapped it around us.

"Don't let go of me," he said.

I looked back. Duke was standing there, blood dripping down the side of his face, wielding a gun.

He helped me.

He helped us.

"Duke!" I screamed. "Hurry!"

He stepped forward, toward us. Pirates clustered around him. He went down. I saw the struggle of the men, a rumble of bodies all moving frantically in the sand. I couldn't see Duke. I didn't know what was happening.

Then I saw the suitcase sitting a few feet away, near the table where they played poker. I ripped myself free and ignored Nash's outraged cry. I grabbed up the suitcase and sprinted back to the ladder where Nash told me I was stupid and then held me tight.

The helicopter began to move. It began to lift us up away from the ground, into the sky.

"Duke!" I screamed one last time.

A final gunshot rang out.

Nash and I stared down as the tangle of pirates separated, leaving a lone body in the sand.

It was Duke.

His chest was saturated in red. He was unmoving.

He was dead.

I turned my face into Nash's chest. His arm tightened around me as the helicopter swung up into the sky and we dangled between safety and the ocean.

The ladder began to tow upward, and long minutes later, we were both sprawled across the floor of the helicopter.

"Are you Ava and Nash?" one of the rescuers asked.

"Yes!" Nash yelled over the engine. "Our plane crashed on the island."

"We saw your smoke flare," the man yelled, passing us thick, heavy blankets. "We had to turn back because of the storm last night."

I wrapped the blanket around me with trembling fingers. I couldn't get the image of Duke out of my head. He hadn't deserved that.

"We flew out this morning before it started to rain again. We were about to head back when we saw the second flare."

"Thank God you came," Nash said. I heard him tell the guy about the pirates. I heard the pilot radio to someone that we were found and that assistance was needed on the unnamed island. He gave coordinates that I didn't understand.

Nash came close, wrapping his blanket around me and then tucking me against his chest. He propped us both up against the wall of the helicopter as we flew away to a nearby island, to a hospital where they apparently were waiting for us.

I tipped my head back, angling it against his chest and looking up at his face.

He kissed me, right on the lips, in front of everyone. "We made it," he whispered, his lips brushing mine.

"I was so afraid you died."

"I wasn't about to die. I have too much to live for."

I rode the rest of the way wrapped in his arms. The relief I felt was insurmountable.

Finally. We were safe.

THE HOSPITAL...

23

Being back among civilization was startling.
Overwhelming.
Loud.
Sounds pinged around inside my brain and pressed in on me, making me want to slap my hands over my ears and yell. I was used to the soft sound of crashing beach waves, the singing cadence of cicadas, and the rush of a falling waterfall.

But sitting in a hospital, none of those sounds could be heard. Instead, I was thrust into a spinning world of beeping, laughter, and coughing. The strong smell of antiseptic and bleach burned my nose and the air-conditioner made my fingers stiff with cold.

The bright lights overhead seemed more intrusive than the sun, and I wished for a pair of sunglasses to shield my eyes.

But I had nothing here with me. Except for the suitcase containing Kiki. Everything that survived the crash was left behind on that island.

I wondered what would become of those pirates. The authorities were called. The Coast Guard was notified. There might not be much law out at sea, but I knew those men would pay for their crimes. Maybe not all of them, but at least for what they did to Duke.

Duke.

He pretended to be our friend. He got close to me with the intention of trading me in for his own safety—his own life. It was so dishonorable that it made me sick.

Yet, I couldn't hate him for it.

He was tortured, abused, robbed of every comfort he'd ever known at the hands of those pirates. He was a victim too. He was only doing what he'd been brainwashed to do, what he thought would get him freedom.

I hoped in death he found the freedom he desperately wanted.

Yes, he was robbed of life, but perhaps being at peace would help make up for that.

It started as a way to survive... but then I realized I couldn't live with myself if you died.

It was his way of apologizing or telling me he knew what he did was wrong. Perhaps in his effort to tempt me away from Nash, he found himself being the one who was tempted. Maybe we reminded him of the life he used to have. Maybe all the talk of us getting home together gave him a spark of hope he thought he lost.

I would never know for sure.

A doctor in a pair of green scrubs and a stethoscope around his neck entered my little room. He gave me a smile and I did my best to return it. "I hear you've had quite an adventure," he said.

[213]

"Is Nash okay?" I asked, not wanting to even act like what we experienced was something out of a movie. It wasn't.

"The man who was brought in with you?"

I nodded.

"He's fine. He's being looked at by another doctor as we speak."

A little bit of the stiffness in my body lessened. I could handle this place if I knew he was okay.

"I'm just going to take a look at those stitches," the doctor said, snapping on a pair of white gloves.

His fingers probed through my hair and I gritted my teeth. His touch wasn't the touch I was used to. It wasn't familiar; it didn't feel good. I didn't really want a stranger to touch me, but I tilted my head down and let the doctor do what he needed to do.

"That's a nasty gash," he said. "You're lucky you're friend was able to close it up. He even saved your hair."

I glanced up. "My hair?"

The doctor pulled his hands away and reached for a tray filled with instruments (instruments = torture). "Yes, if you would have come here with that head wound, we would have shaved the hair around it before we stitched it."

My eyes widened. "Are you going to do that now?"

He laughed. "No need. It's already healed. I am going to take the stitches out and make sure there are no signs of infection."

When I didn't say anything, he picked up a pair of scissors. "You might feel a slight tugging sensation."

He removed my stitches and then examined the wound. Then he assessed the rest of me, asking me a hundred questions. By the time he was done, I was annoyed and exhausted.

The doctor promised to get my discharge papers and then left the room. I was only too happy to see him go.

Before the door swung closed, Nash slipped inside.

"How's the head?" he asked, coming up to the table I was sitting on.

"Good as new," I replied. Suddenly, the noise and the chaos of the hospital didn't seem so bad.

Gently, he turned my head so he could see the area he stitched. These were the hands I was used too. When he was done looking, he dropped a kiss to the top of my head. "Looks good."

"Did they say you could go too?"

He nodded.

"Thank goodness. This place is loud."

He chuckled. "It's going to get louder," he warned.

"What do you mean?"

The door opened and my mother and father burst into the room. "Ava! Oh my God, we thought you were dead," my mother cried.

I sat there in shock. They'd flown all the way from Miami to this hospital in Bermuda?

Nash stepped out of the way just in time to avoid her arms as she crushed me in a bear hug. "Hi, Mom," I squeaked, returning her hug while struggling to breathe.

"We were so worried for you! What you must have gone through! All alone on that island."

"I wasn't completely alone," I said, pulling away and glancing at Nash.

That earned him a crushing hug. "Oh, are you the one who saved my Ava?"

Dad gave me an apologetic look and then offered me a hug of his own. "Glad to have you back, pumpkin," he whispered in my ear.

Tears pricked my eyes. "Glad to be back." I breathed in the familiar scent of him.

"Young man," my father said to Nash, holding out his hand. Nash took it and they shook.

"Dad, this is Nash. Nash, this is my dad."

"You the pilot?" my dad asked, eyeing him.

"Yes, sir."

He made a harrumphing sound and I rolled my eyes. "Dad, Nash kept me alive. He stitched up my head," I explained, poking at the scar I now sported.

"Stitches!" my mother wailed.

She was dramatic.

She should be on soap operas.

"Yes, Mom. But the doctor says I'm fine." I gave Nash a look, trying to tell him that I wasn't about to tell them what else happened on that island.

My mother could do a one-woman show with all that drama.

He seemed to understand and nodded perceptively.

"How did you know we were here?" I asked my father.

"We've been in contact with the search and rescue and the Coast Guard from the beginning. When they first saw the smoke flare, they contacted us and we flew out immediately."

"How did you know it was us?"

"We didn't."

But he had hoped. I gave him a watery smile.

The door opened yet again and more people filed into the room. This time it was the woman from the picture with my grandmother, Nash's abuela. She was followed by a woman with long, dark curly hair and green eyes. Behind her was a tall man with lighter brown hair. I knew right away it was his parents. He looked a lot like his mother.

"Nash!" his abuela cried and then broke into rapid-fire Spanish that made my head spin. I watched him, wondering if he understood what the heck she was saying.

He smiled and nodded. Then he returned her monologue with one of his own—matching her speed.

Wow. He really talked slow to me on that island. And I still hadn't understood.

Before I could ponder that further, he finished talking, and all eyes swung to me. His mother and grandmother both converged, wrapping me in a hug at the same time. They started talking and exclaiming in Spanish once more, and I sat there in the center of them, feeling like I was starring in some sitcom on TV.

"Mom," Nash said with a laugh. "Ava doesn't speak Spanish."

His mother pulled back and looked at me with tears in her eyes. She stroked the side of my cheek with her hand and I actually saw affection in her eyes. *"Bella,"* she murmured.

"Sí," Nash replied. "She's very beautiful."

His grandmother kissed me. "You look like your abuela."

That was the first time anyone ever told me that. I started to cry.

Everyone started talking at once. People were patting my back. My mother was going on about some movie about people who talked to coconuts when they were stranded.

"Everybody out!" Nash yelled over the chaos.

Everyone stopped talking and looked at him. "We love you all. We can't wait to spend time with you. But we need a minute."

To my surprise, they left. My father was the last to go, pressing a kiss to my head. Then he gave Nash an approving look and shut the door behind him.

I collapsed against the table. "It's like a circus."

He chuckled. "Your mother seemed nice."

I burst out laughing. "Tell her that she should have been an actress and she will love you forever."

"So what now?" he said, his voice taking on a serious tone.

It was the question I'd been dreading since we first crashed onto that island. Probably because I knew what I had to do, what this would come to if we ever made it out alive.

Part of me actually wished we had been able to stay there. Even with everything that happened, things on that island seemed simpler.

"Hey," he said softly, coming up and wrapping his arms around my chilled frame. "Why don't we go to the hotel? Shower, get some food. Then we'll talk."

I snuggled into him a little closer, taking a deep breath. He still smelled like the ocean.

"Okay," I replied, my answer muffled against his shirt.

I wasn't used to him wearing a shirt.

"Where'd you get the shirt?" I asked.

He grinned. "One of the nurses gave it to me."

Damn nurses were probably checking him out.

"Come on," he said, lifting me down off the table. I was so incredibly tired all of the sudden.

"The doctor didn't bring my paperwork back."

"We'll sic your mother on him."

I laughed.

He reached for the knob on the door and then stopped. He spun, grabbing me by the shoulders, and looked so far into my eyes I wondered if he saw my soul.

"We're going to be okay," he whispered. "Even if it takes a while."

He kissed me.

It was our first kiss that wasn't on a beach. Our first kiss in the "real world." It was everything it always was: hot, consuming, and deep. I curled my hands into his T-shirt, gripping the cotton fabric tightly. He turned his head one way and then the other, covering every angle he could. His mouth was an onslaught to my already overwhelmed senses. Kissing him was something I would never ever get enough of.

Yet...

Yet this felt like the last time.

It was like we were saying good-bye.

Like when he gazed into my eyes, into my soul, he saw exactly what I tried to hide, exactly what I refused to admit.

And it was like he was telling me it was okay.

The kiss ended too soon. We stood there, bodies pressed together, my hands still tangled in his shirt. He kissed my nose. He kissed my forehead.

"You ready?" he asked, hoarse.

No. "Yes."

He opened the door and stepped out into the hallway. I didn't move. My feet were glued to the floor. I knew the minute we walked out of this room, everything would change.

When I didn't follow, he turned back. He gazed at me so tenderly I literally felt my heart crack.

"Bella," he murmured, stoking my hair. "I know what you're thinking."

"You do?" My voice trembled.

"Yes. You think we need to go our separate ways."

The crack deepened a little bit more. "What if what we feel…?" I gestured between us. "What if it was all just a product of our environment? Two people trying to survive?"

"Do you really think that?" He bent down a little to look directly into my eyes.

"I don't know," I whispered, upset. I was confused. I was overwhelmed. The crash hadn't seemed like that big of a deal on the island. Now, it felt like my life was split in two.

Before and *after.*

In some odd way, I felt like I was getting a fresh start, a do-over of sorts. It seemed like I needed to really think about my life, my feelings, and not just shuffle through the next part of my life. In a way, that crash killed the old me, and in her place was a woman who was ready to take on life and make it what she wanted it to be.

Did I want Nash?

So much it hurt.

But jumping into something seemed wrong. It seemed like I needed to find my... land legs. Like I had spent all this time at sea and I needed to get my balance again on land.

It seemed the fair thing would be to let him go.

They say if you love something—someone—you should set them free...

I felt like being a hoarder.

He took my face in his hands. "I'm going to give you some space, *bella*. The time I think you need."

"But what if I need you too?"

He smiled. "Don't worry. You haven't seen the last of me."

Then he walked me down the hallway, placing me in the arms of my father. Both our families filed out of the hospital, toward the waiting cabs at the curb.

Nash and I were the last to get into our separate cars.

Our eyes met. I watched his dark, unruly head disappear inside the car. His cab drove away. I sat down beside my mother.

We survived a plane crash.

We survived a band of pirates.

We survived a frenemy.

But it seemed the biggest challenge we would face was the one that presented after our rescue...

Reality.

ONE MONTH
LATER...

24

I glanced at the clock and did a double take. Seemed like I just got here and already it was time to leave.

Time flies, I mused, placing the last stem into a gorgeous blown glass vase. I carried it over to the giant glass-front cooler and placed it inside, where it would stay fresh and gorgeous until tomorrow morning's delivery.

After I cleaned up a little around the back, I reluctantly grabbed my bag and stepped out onto the sidewalk. It was fall but much too early for it to feel that way in Miami. More than likely, the temperatures wouldn't even begin to cool off until mid- to late-October. And even when part of the East Coast was buried in snow, Miami would remain mild.

I walked slowly to the bus stop, in no real hurry to get home. In truth, the only time that went by fast was the time I spent at work. Every other second, minute, hour of the day seemed to drag by.

Nighttime was the worst.

I pushed away those thoughts and rode the bus home, trying not to think about the island, Duke, and the nights I spent in the sand... with Nash.

It wasn't until I arrived home and leaned against the back of the door that I finally let myself have the thought.

The thought that plagued me every day.

The thought that echoed around inside me even when I tried not to listen.

The thought I knew was never going to go away.

I missed him.

I missed Nash so much that I could barely breathe. At first, I thought the reason my appetite didn't come back, the reason anxiety sometimes gripped me and threatened to never let go was because of the crash, because of the pirates.

But it wasn't those things.

One day I was in the grocery store, pondering a display of coconuts, when someone behind me called out *bella*, the word sounding exactly as he said it. So many feelings crashed over me in a single second.

Joy.

Desire.

Longing.

Love.

I spun around so fast that all the coconuts tumbled off the table and rolled around my feet. Yet I barely noticed. My eyes searched for his face, for his curls, for the arms that held me for so many nights.

But it wasn't him.

It was someone else.

I stood there completely shattering apart as I watched a woman with dark hair run into the arms of a man that was not Nash.

I left the coconuts on the floor and I went home without whatever I went to the store for in the first place. And I cried. I cried so much my eyes swelled.

And that's when I understood. I knew it wasn't the fact that we survived the awful experience together. It wasn't the fact that we bonded in a crisis.

I loved him in spite of those things.

I loved him because there was no one else that would ever make me feel the way he did.

I did exactly what I told myself I wasn't going to do anymore. I let fear rule my head. I denied my heart because I was afraid to follow it.

I was stupid.

But knowing that couldn't erase the fact that I pushed him away. That I told him we needed time apart to really know if what was between us was real. He'd agreed. Easily. Did that mean he thought I was right? Did that mean I'd been nothing but someone to chase away the boredom while we were stranded on that island?

I sighed and pushed away from the door. It'd been a month since I'd seen him last... two weeks since I realized that my love for him wasn't going to go away. I couldn't go on this way.

I didn't want to live in limbo anymore.

I went into my bedroom and changed out of my work clothes and pulled on a pair of black leggings and a light-green tank top (okay, so yeah, it reminded me of his eyes). Then I reached for a light oversized sweater and tossed it onto my perfectly made bed.

I pulled the band out of my hair and loosened the French braid it was styled in, letting it wave softly down my back. Just as I was reaching for the sweater, there was a knock at the front door.

I frowned, wondering who on Earth that could be, and padded through the living room to throw the lock and pull open the door.

Dark curls and green eyes greeted me.

My heart literally stopped beating.

I reached out and gripped the doorframe, unable to speak. I could only stare.

He looked as good as I remembered him, standing there in low-slung ratty jeans with too many holes. His T-shirt wasn't gray, but a deep green that accentuated his jade-colored stare—a stare that searched my face like a hungry man searching for his final meal.

His skin was still deeply tan, unlined, and the beard he'd been sporting when I said good-bye was gone, revealing his square jaw and the dimple in his chin.

I swallowed, my heart stuttering back to life. "Nash?"

"She remembers my name," he quipped, giving me a little grin. He was carrying a large cardboard box with the words *Pizza Hut* scrawled along the side.

My stomach roared to life fiercely.

"Is that a pizza?" I asked.

"Large veggie with pan crust."

Tears rushed to my eyes, blurring my vision and making it hard to stare at him. "You remembered." When we first crashed, it was the one food I told him I wanted.

"I know you probably have eaten a million of these since you got home…" he said and shrugged as his words died away.

I shook my head. "I haven't had it yet."

His eyes zeroed in on my face. "You haven't?"

I shook my head again. Of course I hadn't. I couldn't eat something that reminded me so fully of him.

"You gonna let me in?" he asked, devastating me with his lopsided grin.

I stepped back, gesturing for him to come in, and then shut the door behind him. He looked around the apartment with rapt interest. His eyes took in the cream walls, the oversized posters filled with art and landscapes, the gray couch with multi-colored pillows, and the coffee table scattered with a million magazines (and not one of them managed to take my mind off him).

"Nice place," he said, his eyes sweeping over me from head to toes.

"Thanks," I echoed, realizing that I looked like I was ready to curl up on the couch and eat an entire pint of ice cream in front of some cheesy Lifetime movie.

Well, that's what I was going to do. But still.

"I'll be right back," I said and rushed from the room.

In my bedroom, I leaned against the wall, trying to catch my breath, trying to calm the pounding of my heart. He was here. He was standing in my living room. He was so close I could reach out and touch him.

Lust erupted inside me. Just the mere thought of putting my hands anywhere on his body had me practically salivating. I rushed to my closet to look inside, but I never got the chance to debate my wardrobe because a quiet sob racked my body.

I leaned into the frame, against the open door, as tears rolled down my cheeks.

[227]

I felt a hand on my elbow, gentle at first but then his grip tightening. *"Bella,"* he said softly.

My quiet sob broke and I spun, burying my face in his chest. His arms came around me instantly, holding me so tight it almost hurt. But I liked it because I knew he was there.

After long moments of me blubbering all over him, I quieted and he pulled me back, tipping up my chin and staring into my tearstained face.

"You missed me."

"Every. Single. Day."

"Thank God," he groaned and pressed his forehead against mine. "I was afraid when I got here you would tell me that you hadn't."

"I never should never have let you leave."

"I know."

"But you didn't give up."

"Someone told me once that when you love someone you should never give up."

"What did you say?" I whispered, not sure I heard him right.

"I love you, *bella*."

My heart swelled to the point I thought my ribs wouldn't be able to contain it. "I love you too. So much."

His kiss swept me up into a tidal wave of passion, washing away an entire month's worth of longing. My body remembered everything about him and fit itself against him perfectly, knowing exactly where to go. My fingers went for his curls, tangling in their softness, and my tongue rushed inside his mouth as if it would rather be there than inside mine.

The softness of his T-shirt brushed against my arms, and while it was comforting, there was something else I would rather feel. I delved below his hem, gripping the skin of his taut waist and moaning.

He ripped his mouth away and tugged the shirt up and over his head, throwing it across the room, and then was on me again in seconds. He backed me up against the wall and used his body to pin me there as his mouth traveled hotly over my neck and collarbone.

He reached up and pulled down the straps of my tank top, ripping the bodice completely down my waist and exposing every ounce of my aching flesh. My breasts were already swelling with need and I shoved myself out, gripping his head and bringing it down to one of my sensitive nipples. He nipped at it with his teeth and I cried out.

As he kissed and sucked, I found the waistband of his jeans and pulled it away, delving my hands inside his boxers to find the object of my desire. It was pulsing and ready. His entire body jerked when I closed my hand around him.

"This is going to be fast," he said against my breast. "I've missed you too badly to drag it out."

"Do it," I growled, giving his member a squeeze.

In a blurred frenzy, our clothes hit the floor and we fell backward on the bed. Nash rolled, tucking me beneath him and sinking himself immediately in my moist heat.

Both of us groaned and stilled as pure pleasure rolled over us.

And then we were moving, slapping against each other with intense fervor. The orgasm ripped through my body, and I cried out his name over and over again until my insides stopped quaking. And then it was his turn. With one final thrust, he pulsed inside me, emptying everything he had into my more-than-willing body.

Long after we were finished, my muscles continued to contract around him, squeezing him and making him flex inside me.

"Damn," he said, tucking me into his side. "You have no idea how badly I've been wanting to do that."

"I think I might."

He chuckled and then dragged us farther up the bed, seeing as how our feet were dangling off. I guess we should be lucky we made it onto the bed at all.

"Uh, Ava?" he said after he settled me into his side once more.

"Yes?"

"Where are your pillows?"

I lifted an arm and pointed over to the side of the bed. He paused and then sat up, glancing over the mattress and down onto the floor.

"You mind explaining to me why you have a pile of blankets and pillows on the floor?"

"I've been sleeping there."

He took my cheek in his hand and looked down, concern lacing his eyes. "Baby, are you still having nightmares? You should have called me."

I shook my head, silencing his words. "I can't sleep in this bed."

"Why?"

"It's too soft..." I murmured.

He looked confused, and then realization dawned. "You're used to sleeping on the floor or on the beach."

"With you," I whispered. "I tried to sleep here, but I just couldn't. It was too soft and too... lonely."

He settled back against the mattress. "How's it feel right now?"

"Perfect," I said, sighing.

And then my stomach had to go and ruin it all by growling.

He laughed. "It sounds like you're hungry." His hands caressed my hip and up my ribs. "And you actually feel like you've lost weight."

"I haven't gotten my appetite back yet," I mumbled.

He bounded off the bed, not bothering with pants, and I was treated to the epic view of his tight ass sauntering out into the living room. When he returned carrying the pizza, I was treated to another epic view... of his front side.

He set the pizza on the foot of the bed and retrieved a giant slice oozing with white cheese and piled high with veggies. He sat down, holding out the slice. "Eat," he demanded.

I loved when he bossed me around.

I took a bite.

It was really good.

We sat that way in the quiet of my apartment, not talking, just him feeding me bite after bite of pizza. Only after I ate the last bite did he get a slice for himself (which he ate in like three seconds).

"I need to tell you something," I said, nerves crackling along my spine.

"That sounds serious."

I nodded.

"Something happened on the island."

"A lot of things happened on the island."

"Something I was afraid to tell you about."

"You don't have to be afraid to tell me anything, *bella*."

I wondered if he would say that even after I told him. "You know how I was having those dreams?"

He nodded. "The nightmares about the crash."

"They weren't nightmares about the crash." I paused. "Well, the first one was."

"What were the other ones about?"

"Me and you…" I let the sentence end suggestively.

A slow smile formed on his face.

I held up my hand. "But it wasn't just me and you."

He frowned. "What do you mean?"

"I mean there was someone else in the dream with us… doing things."

"Please tell me it was another girl."

Only a man would pray for that…

"It wasn't."

He looked like he was punched in the gut. "It was *him*, wasn't it?"

I nodded, tears forming in my eyes. Geesh, I was turning into an emotional basket case. Maybe I should stock up on tissues. "I don't know why." I sniffled. "I felt so guilty."

"Why would you feel guilty, *bella*?" he said softly, caressing the side of my face. I leaned into his touch.

"It felt like I was betraying you somehow."

"You didn't actually sleep with him… like on the island?" he said, watching me.

I shook my head adamantly. "Only you. There's been only you."

"Even since you came home?" he asked, his voice a little strained.

"There will only ever be you."

He let out a breath.

"What about you? Since we've been home?" My stomach cramped. The thought of him with anyone else made me physically ill.

"No, *bella*, just you." He threaded our fingers together. "I had to fight myself constantly not to come here and bang on your door."

"You did?"

He nodded. "I just wanted to give you the time you needed. I wanted you to be sure."

"I've never been so sure."

"That's real good because I'm never doing this again. I'm moving in. You're going to stop sleeping on the floor and start sleeping in my arms."

Like I said, I loved his bossiness.

"You're going to move in? What about Puerto Rico? What about being a pilot?"

"I can be a pilot from here. We can visit Puerto Rico." He glanced at the urn I still had yet to part with. "We can start with putting Kiki to rest. The way she deserves."

"I'd like that."

He grabbed another slice of pizza and stuck it under my nose. I dutifully took a bite.

"What have you been up to since you got home?"

"I got a new job. One I really love."

"Doing what?" he asked gently, tucking the hair behind my ear.

"I'm a florist. A flower design specialist," I said around a bite of cheesy goodness. "I work at a local flower shop, putting together bouquets and arrangements."

He smiled.

"I don't have to sit behind a desk. I don't have to do math. I get to stare at beautiful flowers all day and make bows with gorgeous ribbons."

"I'm glad you found something you love."

I nodded. "Someday I want to open my own shop. I already have a name."

He raised an eyebrow.

"*Bella Flora*," I pronounced, totally butchering the Spanish language.

Nash repeated it. It sound incredibly romantic on his tongue. "I like it."

"Me too."

"And I love you."

"I love you more."

"You're not mad about the dreams?"

"I can't say I'm thrilled about it. You with another man is kind of my own personal nightmare."

"I didn't have sex with him in the dream. He just kissed me and stuff."

"And then what?"

"And then you pulled me away."

"This is where you belong, *bella*." He pulled me into his lap, cradling me against his chest.

"I'm so glad we didn't just have traumatic bonding."

He stilled. "What?"

"I Googled it. That's what it's called when people get close through trauma."

He muttered under his breath, "You Googled it." Then louder he said, "You should have looked up post traumatic stress disorder. Only a girl suffering from that would push away a catch like me."

I stifled a laugh. "Hmmm. Maybe I should look that up." I made a move to get up.

His grip tightened and he growled. "No more Google."

I kissed the underside of his chin. "Deal."

"If you ever want to know how I feel, just ask me. I'm more than willing to tell you."

"I think I can tell how you're feeling right now," I murmured, desire thick in my voice.

His growing erection nudged me again. "It's not morning, *bella*," he whispered, making goose bumps rise along my arms. "It's all you."

"We have lost time to make up for," I said, turning in his lap, sinking down onto him instantly.

"By all means," he said, gripping my hips and rocking me across his hardness. "Get to work."

A *very* long time later, I fell asleep, not on the floor, but in his arms. A place I planned to sleep for the rest of my life.

Just before slipping away, a thought of Duke drifted over my mind. I pushed it away, unwilling to let a dead man who tried to kill us tempt me away from happiness. I knew that vowing to never think of him again was fruitless. What he did was something that couldn't be forgotten. But not letting those thoughts consume me was something I *could* do.

The last thought I had before sleep claimed me completely was that controlling my thoughts was a lot easier than controlling my dreams…

I came awake with soft caresses. Barely there touches that glided over my skin, making me hyper aware of every single thing I felt.

My eyes were heavy—from sleep, from lust. I kept them closed, allowing the sensations of his hands and mouth to consume me. I could get used to this… to wake up to this every single day.

His tongue circled my belly button, and then he scattered kisses across my belly and landed on my hip. He pressed his slightly open mouth to the hollowed area between my hip and my pelvis, making my hips lurch upward and my hands search for his head.

"More," I whispered, my sleepy voice tinged with pleading.

He kissed lower, burying his nose and mouth in my short, springy curls, all the while his mouth sliding lower. I opened my legs for him. They were already trembling. He gripped the outside of my hips and yanked me forward so the most secret place of me collided with his mouth.

I groaned. His tongue began to work me into a tizzy. I grasped for him but couldn't quite reach as new sensations rolled over me and I fell back against the sheets once more, submitting to every single thing he made me feel.

My foot slid along his waist, cupping his ribcage and urging him closer.

Two fingers tested my soaking wet opening, but I made a sound of protest. "You," I murmured. "I just want you."

He crawled up my body, rubbing along me like a cat, and I moaned again, hooking my legs around his waist.

"Nash," I sighed.

He said nothing.

Something uneasy broke through my heavy desire.

I was dreaming. It was just like before.

Wake up, Ava! *I yelled at myself.*

But it seemed the dream had me in its grip. I was torn. I wanted to get away… yet I wanted to continue.

Please, not again. *The thought whimpered through my mind.*

Finally, we were together. The island was behind us. The dreams were behind… Duke was gone.

"Open your eyes," the man above me whispered.

I squeezed them shut harder and shook my head. If it wasn't Nash, I would never forgive myself. I would be haunted forever with the dreams about another man. A man I most certainly didn't want, but seemed to have the ability to kidnap my dreams.

A large, warm hand closed over my breast. I arched up off the bed. So good...

No! Stop that! *I yelled at myself.*

Then he gripped my nipple and twisted it just lightly. Pleasure tingled through every ounce of me.

"Look at the man your heart truly desires," the man whispered again.

I tried to decipher his voice. I couldn't. I was so upset and caught between dream ad reality I didn't know what to do.

There was only one thing I could do.

I took a breath.

And opened my eyes.

I blinked, adjusting to the dim lighting, and nervously looked up at the man who was hovering over me, ready to take me.

It was Nash.

"Bella," he whispered when my eyes collided with his.

Relief so strong poured over me as Nash reached out to stroke my cheek. And then he entered me in one long, hard stroke.

I took his face in my hands and stared up at him. Overjoyed with this man. My heart and body was so full of him that there was no room for anyone else.

There was only him.

In my heart. In my dreams. In my forever.

THE END

Cambria Hebert

Today is your lucky day! Not only did you get to read TEMPT, but now you get an exclusive sneak peak of TEXT, the next *Take It Off* novel, coming November 2013!

One text can change everything.

Honor Calhoun never thought her life would ever be like the books she writes for a living. One morning while out for a run, she learns plot twists aren't only found in novels. Some horrors can actually come true.

She faces off with a persistent attacker, holds her own, but in the end is taken hostage and thrown into a hole. In the middle of the woods.

But Honor didn't go down there alone.

She took her kidnapper's phone with her. With a spotty signal and a dying battery, her hope is slim.

Nathan Reed is an active duty Marine stationed at a small reservist base in Pennsylvania. All he wants is a calm and uneventful duty station where he can forget the memories of his time in a war-torn country.

But a single text changes everything.

Nathan becomes Honor's only hope for survival, and he has to go against the clock, push aside his past, and take on a mission for a girl he's never met.

Both of them want freedom... but they have to survive long enough to obtain it.

You ready for the goods? Turn the page!

TEXT

Sneak Peek

1

Honor

Early morning sunlight filtered through the overhead canopy of burnished autumn leaves, and crisp, chilled air brushed over my cheeks, filling my lungs with every deep inhale I took. My hot-pink Nikes pounded lightly against the gravel path on which I ran, and the sound of Mackelmore filled my ears.

I loved this time of day. It was just me, the trail, and the exertion of my muscles. Running was something I knew I would always do. It was my escape. It was my way of de-stressing, of letting my mind wander wherever it wanted. I didn't have to think about deadlines, or emails, or dealing with people. I was in the moment, working my body and releasing all the tension and stress that built up inside me during the day.

I took a second to wipe my brow and then glanced up. A light breeze ruffled the trees and leaves rained down around me, littering the already covered path. I could barely see the gravel because so many had already fallen. It was absolutely gorgeous. It motivated me to run farther, to run longer, because being out here, in the purest form of nature during the fall, was close to heaven for me.

To my right, a creek flowed, the water rushing over rocks insistently like it was racing me. Plants and trees grew along the bank, jutting into the moving water. Leaves were carried along with the current, dotting the dark water with bright spots of yellow and orange. Occasionally, a fish would jump up and splash, leaving ripples in its wake.

This trail stretched for thirty miles. Thirty miles of scenic pleasure. Thirty miles of untouched wilderness that blended in naturally with the mountainous small town where I made my home. This trail was the main reason I moved here. I felt so close to nature, so at peace. Whenever I had a bad day, I could go down to the creek or walk along the path and be instantly calmed. This place had a way of reminding me how life was bigger than just me, how I shouldn't get so caught up in the everyday that I forget to enjoy the beauty around me.

I glanced down at the pedometer strapped to my upper arm. I'd already gone over three miles. I needed to turn back. By the time I made it back to my house, I would be over six miles for the day.

Oh well. This long run earned me a big fat dessert or maybe a pizza later.

I turned and started back the way I came, toward my little house that sat right along the trail. Some spots of the path were more isolated than others. I was running along in a place that had no homes around it, but in about another mile, I would start passing a few and a small row of townhouses.

I rounded the bend in the path and ran over a wooden bridge that carried me atop the rushing creek and then back into the gravel. The trees and wildlife grew right up to the path here. It was dense and full. In another month or so, it would look more bare, the leaves would be mostly gone, and I would be able to see farther back into the woods. But not today. Today the plants provided ample coverage.

Unfortunately.

As I ran, something darted out from the side. I jerked, the sudden movement startling me. My stride faltered and I turned toward whatever it was, but I didn't see it.

It plowed into me, knocking me over, my hip taking the brunt of my fall. I grunted in pain and scrambled to get up.

But someone pinned me down.

I shoved at the man, and he glanced down, his eyes meeting mine. There was something cold in his blue-eyed stare. Something empty and flat.

Panic bloomed in my chest, spiking through my body as my heart rate went wild and alarm bells started sounding in my head.

Yes, I read the stories. Yes, I saw it on the news. *Woman is kidnapped. Search for missing woman continues. Woman is found beaten and dead.*

But that stuff didn't happen to *me*. That stuff happened to other people. Unfortunate women… women that weren't me.

This isn't happening to me.

A surge of adrenaline had me bringing my knee up and catching the man in his balls. He made a high-pitched sound and fell to the side. I scrambled up and took off, racing down the path, toward the road that

intersected it. If I could make it there, I could flag
down a car. I could find someone to help me.

The earbuds had fallen out of my ears and hung
around my neck, banging into my skin and reminding
me that I had my phone. My phone! As I ran, my
hand fumbled, trying to yank it out of the band
around my arm. Finally, I managed to grasp it and I
held it up in front of me, calling up the keypad and
dialing.

9-1—

He tackled me from behind and I fell face
forward, the phone tumbling out of my hands, just
ahead, just out of reach. I cried out and stretched my
hand toward my lifeline, desperate to finish the call.

"You're going to pay for that, bitch," the gruff
voice said.

I'd never known such fear in all my life. I could
barely think straight. Straight-laced dread and panic
took over my body, making my limbs feel heavy and
numb.

Don't give in, the voice inside me screamed.

I bucked like a pony and reached forward, my
hand closing over my phone. *Yes!* My joy was
extremely short-lived when the man, who was still
straddling my back, snatched it out of my hand and
tossed it into the nearby creek.

"No," I cried, watching it swept away beneath
the surface.

"No one's going to help you," the voice above
intoned.

Something inside me went deadly calm. Like the
fear and panic flat lined, leaving behind nothing but
the sound of my deep, even breathing.

This fucker had no idea who he was dealing with.

I grabbed a handful of gravel beside my face and threw it behind me, right at the man. He didn't tumble off me, but he did swear and I felt him fidget about. I grabbed another handful and launched it at him as I pushed up on my hands and knees, forcing my way out from beneath him.

When I got to my feet, he grabbed me around the ankle and yanked me back. I reached into the hidden zippered pocket of my pants and pulled out a small container of mace. I carried it in case I ran into a bear or some aggressive animal.

I should have known that the real thing to be afraid of out here was another human being.

I flipped the little cap and depressed the button, the spray shooting forward.

But it missed him. He was still low to the ground.

Still clutching the mace, I took off running. I got maybe three steps when he tackled me again. Gravel cut into my cheek and stung my hands.

I started to scream.

I yelled as loud as I could.

He flipped me over and slapped a hand over my mouth. His face was dirty from the gravel and dust I flung at him. His eyes were no longer so empty... They were now filled with excitement.

I glanced down and noticed the tent in his pants, and I gagged.

He was sick. This was sick. This couldn't be happening to me.

"Shut. Up," he said and rocked against me.

I bit him.

He howled in pain and snatched away his hand. As I screamed, I reached out and grabbed at the erection that made me gag and yanked on it, twisting it, digging in my nails and hoping the pain would immobilize him enough for me to get free once more.

In the distance, a dog was barking, and I prayed that meant someone was headed this way, someone that would help me.

My attacker slapped his hand over my mouth again. The taste of blood, metallic and sharp, had me recoiling. His legs were shaking and I knew he was in pain.

But it hadn't been enough.

I saw it in his face.

I felt it in my bones.

I wasn't getting away.

I tried to buck him off one last time. I reached out for two more handfuls of gravel and dirt.

He drew back his arm and punched me. Right in the face.

And then there was nothing.

ACKNOWLEDGEMENTS

I really hope you all enjoyed this book. It was one heck of a ride, wasn't it? At times I felt like I was on the plane barreling toward the ocean as I was writing it.

This book is a classic example of how the best laid plans can go awry. It started out with a different title, a title I loved. *Triangle.* I originally planned to write a book about a girl caught between two guys, stranded on an island in the Bermuda triangle. Hence the title *Triangle.* It was an ode to the Bermuda Triangle and to a love triangle. I wanted to do something different with the whole love triangle, because in all honesty... as a reader, I don't like love triangles. They annoy me. And is it just me, or am I the only one who picks the guy who never gets picked? Like seriously?

Then I end up in a corner, sucking my thumb asking the heroine, "Why? Why, would you do this to me?"

Yeah. Not fun.

So I vowed to twist it, to make it better.

Then Nash crashed onto the pages. He had me at the ratty jeans. The moment he threw himself on top of Ava and whispered Spanish in her ear, well... I became his slave.

There was NO WAY in H-E-double hockey sticks that Ava would ever be lured away from such perfection. Am I right, or am I right?

I mean, it seemed almost silly to even have her have feelings for someone else.

And that's where the battle for the plot began.

It was a long battle.

The characters won. I pretty much felt like a loony bin patient with all the thoughts rolling around my head. The Bermuda Triangle was supposed to play a bigger roll... In truth, Duke was supposed to be a ghost.

Yeah, not so much.

Instead, we got pirates, betrayal, and Nash.

Yet, I still hung on to Duke, to the possible love triangle. Only it's not really a love triangle, is it? It was naughty Duke trying to lure Ava away.

Although, in truth, I think Duke had feelings for her. I just think he was crazy in the head. The things he lived through... well, you know. But if they had met on the street, he would have liked her. He would have asked her out.

She would have said no.

But he wouldn't have tried to kill her for it.

Anywho, as you can tell by my above rambling, this book was a challenge to write. The most challenging New Adult Contemporary I have written thus far (okay, fine, it is only my third one—but still). It's the last time I battle the characters over the way I think a plot should go.

It makes me crazy.

They win anyway.

I would like to acknowledge my husband, Shawn Hebert, for laughing when I told him how hard the book was to write. His response? "You say that every time."

So maybe I do. This time I meant it.

Yes, I say that every time too.

Thanks, honey, for listening to me go on about plane crashes, texting you at work about flare guns, and then not laughing when I asked you what you would say if I told you I had a dream about being with two men…

No, I will not tell you what he said.

LOL.

To my daughter, Kaydence, who always keeps it real and tells me that my writing is boring. Who tells me that she wishes she could have a job where one lazed around on FB all day… Even though you say all those things, I know the minute I tell you that you are old enough to read my books, you will do so. And you won't say they are boring. Ha-ha-ha.

To my son Nathan, who distracts me from writing by bringing home stray cats and making me feed them. Who shows me his houses and the zombies on his Minecraft game (I still don't get that game) and who tells me that he likes my books—but he isn't going to read them. Ha-ha.

To Regina Wamba and Cassie McCown. The two ladies who are always there to clean up my messes and make my stuff look pretty.

To Amber Garza and Cameo Renae, always there to cheer me on. And to all the ladies of Indie Inked who know exactly what it's like to be a writer.

Thank you all for buying my books. For reading them. For tweeting me. For posting on your blogs and for leaving a review. You truly are my inspiration.

Tempt

Cambria Hebert is the author of the young adult paranormal *Heven and Hell* series, the new adult *Death Escorts* series, and the new adult *Take it Off* series. She loves a caramel latte, hates math, and is afraid of chickens (yes, chickens). She went to college for a bachelor's degree, couldn't pick a major, and ended up with a degree in cosmetology. So rest assured her characters will always have good hair. She currently lives in North Carolina with her husband and children (both human and furry), where she is plotting her next book. You can find out more about Cambria and her work by visiting http://www.cambriahebert.com.

"Like" her on Facebook:
https://www.facebook.com/pages/Cambria-Hebert/128278117253138
Follow her on Twitter: https://twitter.com/cambriahebert
Pinterest: https://pinterest.com/cambriahebert/pins/
GoodReads:
http://www.goodreads.com/author/show/5298677.Cambria_Hebert
Cambria's website: http://www.cambriahebert.com

Take a look at bestselling author L.P. Dover's newest release.
TRUSTING YOU

Prologue

Three Months Ago

A night at the bar, several tequila sunrises, and a gorgeous guy staring at me from across the room … how could I resist? Talking became flirting, flirting became touching, and then the touching led me to where I was now.

There were only a couple more hours until the first rays of sunshine would alert the coming of dawn. I was angry with myself for letting things go too far with the man sleeping soundly off to my side. How could I be so stupid yet love everything I did?

Sleeping with random men was not something I would ever do, and definitely not something I should be doing now. I was twenty-eight years old and already divorced from my college love, who made the mistake of sleeping with our whore of a neighbor. She'd spread her legs for anyone. Daniel just couldn't resist, and of course I couldn't resist divorcing him when he begged me to give him another chance. Marrying him was a mistake, and I couldn't believe I was stupid enough to think he would stay faithful. After all, I had known of his reputation as a wealthy playboy. He pursued me with a vengeance and I fell hard. *Shame on me once, never twice.*

After our divorce was final, my friends decided it was time I celebrated … and boy did I celebrate. We went out to bars every weekend and I dated many different men, which soon became tiring; they were either too wrapped up in themselves or complete douche bags. I had yet to find a man that was completely interested in who I was, and took the time to put my needs first. At least, until my gaze met the handsome stranger's from across the room of the bar whose bed I now occupied.

My lover for the evening had drifted off to sleep not long after we spent the night rolling around the sheets. Even though he was a one night stand, he sure knew every way possible to make my body scream for his touch; it was intoxicating. It shocked me, but I indulged in the reckless fun for that short amount of time. I felt more wanted and desired in those hours of sex than I had the entire time I was married.

My ex was a good lover, but nothing compared to the passion and heat of the man off to my right. He was sleeping on his stomach, the naked flesh of his back exposed to the moonlight drifting in through the window. His muscled arm was curled under his pillow and his breathing was light and relaxed ... so peaceful, and perfect. Even in his sleep he was one of the most handsome men I'd ever laid eyes on.

No, I scolded silently to myself. He may appear perfect, but I knew better than to fall into the trap of good looks and a charming smile. *I will not be fooled again.*

Slowly slipping out of bed, I gathered up my clothes that were strewn on the floor and quietly put them on, trying my best not to make any sound. I ran my fingers through my auburn waves, but gave up when all I felt were knots. It was going to be a bitch to brush out when I got home.

Before I snuck out of the bedroom, I took one last look at the man who had been the most aggressive and passionate lover I'd ever had. His dark, tousled hair was mussed up from my relentless tugging, and his closed eyes hid the sparkling gray color that glowed the entire time he ravished my body.

I must say ... I didn't regret what had happened with this man, and if I had the chance I'd probably do it again. He lived in a swanky condo in downtown Charlotte which I knew had to cost a fortune. Then again, my experience with wealthy men was tainted by my ex-husband ... although, this man was *nothing* like my ex. It was clear he had money, but he never gloated about it when we talked at the bar. It was refreshing to talk to a man who was confident enough not to brag about himself the whole night.

However, no one was perfect and I knew he had to be far from it.

Shutting the bedroom door with a quiet click, I grabbed my purse off of the kitchen table and started to tiptoe to the front door, but stopped. Pulling out a piece of paper in my purse, I scribbled my number on it and laid it on the kitchen table. *What am I doing?*

I stared at the paper lying there and immediately thought of one word … desperate. And desperate was something I was not. Snatching the paper off of the table, I crumpled it in my hand. The guy was probably a player just like all the other men I'd come across. What made him so special that I'd give in and lower my guard?

Nothing, my mind screamed at me.

Jamming the crinkled paper into my purse, I tiptoed quietly to the front door and slipped out silently. There was one thing for certain, and my heart hated me for it. I wasn't going to forget what happened tonight or the lover that made me orgasm more times in just a few hours than I had in the past year. The ache between my legs was going to remind me for the next couple of days what went on during this raging night of passion. As I sauntered into the elevator, my body screamed for me to go back. It wanted me to indulge in another round of a sex induced high with the man that had me panting for him like no other.

Except, I couldn't go back … my heart wouldn't let me.

Cambria Hebert

Chapter One

It was a Friday afternoon on a hot summer day—one of the last summer days left—and I enjoyed it on my back deck soaking up the sun. It was closing in on fall time, but the way our weather had been here in North Carolina I chose to keep my pool open just a little while longer. It was September and we still had ninety degree days. I prayed every day for a cold winter, but I never got my wish. Hell, I'd love to see snow, but we hadn't gotten that in a couple of years either.

However, lying out by my pool was good for relaxation. Especially after spending the whole day with high schoolers who mainly spent their time secretly texting when they should've been paying attention to their books.

I did decide to give them a break since it was Friday and also the night of the rivalry football game. They were all too excited about that to concentrate on anything else. Even though I never had to work because of all of the money my ex-husband made, I knew I wasn't ever going to sit on my ass and do nothing. Being a high school biology teacher wasn't exactly a money making job, but it was something I was excited about doing. The settlement money I got out of Daniel would keep me afloat for a lifetime without having to work, but I enjoyed being at the school; it made me feel like I was doing something right.

Sweat dripped down my brow as I slipped off my sandals and placed my sunglasses down on the glass table beside my lounge chair. I was about to dive into

[254]

the pool when my phone started buzzing beside my half drunk glass of sweet tea.

I smiled when I saw who it was.

Korinne Matthews was one of my closest friends growing up, and when we both separated to go to different colleges we sort of grew apart. It wasn't until one fateful day when she showed up at my doorstep that our friendship rekindled like no time had passed whatsoever. She was an interior designer who I had made an appointment with to decorate my house, not knowing she was the same Korinne of our childhood. Now we talked almost every day.

"Why hello there, Korinne," I answered happily.

"How are you?" she asked, but then spoke again, "Oh wait … Let me guess, you're sitting by your pool like you do every day when I call you."

I laughed and slipped my sunglasses back on so I wouldn't have to squint. "You know it. Oh yeah, and also avoiding my ex-husband's calls. I think he's apologized over a million times now. He keeps sending me text messages saying he still wants me and loves me."

Korinne scoffed, "When is he going to take the hint? It's been a year now. Please tell me he's not wearing you down."

"Definitely not," I shrieked. "I'll admit I loved him, and he was good to me for a while, until his ego got the better of him. I can't forgive him for cheating on me. It's not going to happen."

"I understand, Mel. So what else is new?"

Gazing out at the pool with its cool water beckoning me, I sighed. "Well, I'm trying to enjoy the last few days of summer now that I have them. Its nice getting home early in the afternoons and spending them out here. I'm looking forward to the fall and winter, though."

"Oh, me too. Watching the leaves change colors at our home in the mountains is the most beautiful sight I've ever seen. Other than my little girl that is."

I smiled. The thought of little Anna-Grace's smiling face as I bounced her in my arms would always stay with me. One day I'd have a child of my own. I was thankful I never got pregnant with Daniel, especially now that we were divorced.

"How is she doing? I bet she misses her Aunt Melissa," I said.

I could hear the baby giggling in the background and Korinne laughed. "Oh, she's doing well. She has her daddy wrapped around her little finger. I swear all she has to do is look at Galen and his heart stops."

Galen, her husband, scoffed in the background and chided into the phone, "Don't let her fool you, Melissa. Korinne's wrapped around Anna-Grace's finger, too."

Korinne chuckled. "Okay, fine, I'm wrapped around her finger, too. I guess it's hard not to when you spend years thinking you can't have kids and then you finally get pregnant. Anyway, the reason why I called is because I wanted to know what you were doing tomorrow night."

Going to bars, I guess, I thought to myself.

"I'm not sure," I said slowly, curious as to why she'd ask. "Why? What do you have in mind?"

"Well," she began, "there's a party tomorrow night and I want you to come. Galen's company is celebrating the expansion of his firm, and I thought it would be something you'd like to take part in. It'll be fun with lots of people." After pausing for a brief second, she delightfully added, "...good people."

I knew that tone and I knew it very well. Korinne had a reason for me going to this party and it wasn't so she could see me. Exasperated, I groaned and muttered, "Kori, seriously. Have you not learned your lesson yet? You need to stop trying to play matchmaker ... I'm not interested. After me telling you no the past few times I thought you would've gotten the hint."

She begged, "Please, Mel, it'll be fun. I've wanted you to meet this guy at our firm for the past couple of months. He's really hot and Galen just hired him as his lead architect for the West Coast accounts. Come on, what else do you have to do tomorrow? If all else fails you can hang out with me the whole time."

I sat in silence for a moment, contemplating. Korinne was a good judge of character, so if she said the guy was a good man I had to believe her, but I couldn't help feeling like I was a charity case. *I can get men on my own.* I just tend to get the wrong ones. It wasn't like Korinne was setting us up on a blind date or anything, and if I didn't want to talk to him I didn't have to.

"Please," she pleaded. I rolled my eyes and hung my head. There was no way I'd get out of it. She would beg me until I gave in.

"Are you going to give me an answer sometime this year?" Korinne asked, snickering.

Sighing, I huffed out a breath and gave in. "Okay, fine. I'll go, but it's not a blind date. I'm going for *you* and you only since you asked me to. I'll meet your friend and that's it. I don't want any expectations you hear me?"

Korinne burst out laughing. "You *are* still the little firecracker that you were in high school. Don't worry though. He has no clue he's meeting you tomorrow either. So whatever you're thinking, I didn't plan on it being a blind date. I just think you need to meet him. He's extremely good looking. Very nice, too."

Well, at least he didn't know about me, which was good. Blind dates were awkward enough without that pressure. "Good. Well let's keep it that way and not tell him about me," I told her. "I don't want you going into detail about my past. You tend to talk too much."

"Hey," she scolded. "You have nothing to worry about, Mel. I don't think he'd want to hear about your loser ex-husband anyway." Korinne's daughter began to fuss in the background. "All right, my lovely friend, the little one needs to be fed and put down for a nap. I'll see you tomorrow night, seven o'clock, at the firm downtown. The party will be on the very top floor, but there'll also be people there to guide you. Dress nice and you better have a smile on your face when I see you."

Grinning, I rolled my eyes and shook my head. "Okay, you have my word. See you then."

We both said our good-byes and hung up. The last thing I wanted to do was let my friend down when she'd done so much for me. *Who knows, I might actually have fun.*